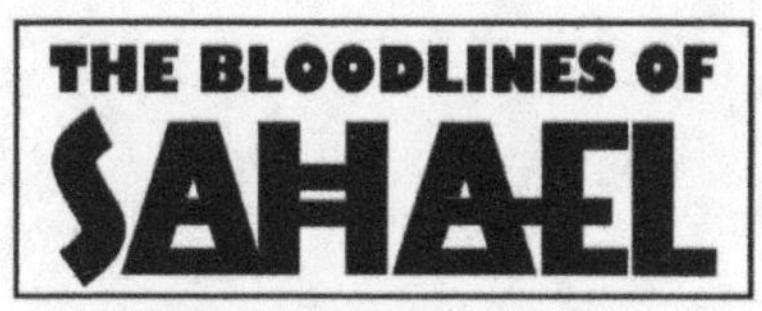

VOLUME ONE

BOOK FOUR

ANCIENT REMNANTS

BY

DWAYNE ANTHONY MADRY

Printed in the United States of America

First Printing, 2024

ISBN 978-1-963089-03-5

Cover Design by JessHavok

www.SAHAEL.com

Intoduction into Sahael

As Iceoth melts away and reveals Nile's ancient flame, Oadira's peaceful life is once again disrupted by the forces of destiny. The power of the flame grants the Black Madonna the ability to assert her influence over all those around her, guiding them on a journey back to Sahael. Oadira, now with a family of her own, must navigate this new chapter in her story, balancing her personal desires with the responsibilities that come with her newfound power.

As she embraces her role as a leader, Oadira is faced with difficult decisions and challenges that will test her strength and resilience. The melting of Iceoth becomes a metaphor for change and transformation, as Oadira and her family embark on a journey towards a new future, guided by the ancient flame that has resurfaced to shape their destinies.

CHAPTER CONTENTS

CHAPTER I

THE OPEN WATERS

Aardian Ocean

The Treep spiders pursued the people through the tunnel, but Oadira focused ahead as they planned to escape through the water and drown the giant arachnids once and for all.

People shouted and cried behind her as many of their family members had already been taken by the spiders during their flight through the tunnels. Oadira could still smell the acidic residue from the Treep's webbing.

Just as Lyshyla had promised, they approached a transparent, sapphire seal, which prevented water from flooding the tunnels entirely. The seal was adorned with a strange symbol that Oadira had never seen before. It was the symbol of the Marula Tree with large branches and roots that connected all the tribes in Alkebulan to the tribes of Sahael. The branches connected to the four empires on the continent of Alkebulan and the horn of Alkebulan.

Oadira put her hand through the transparent barrier and pulled it back after noticing that her hand was wet. Apparently, the seal allowed those of the Chosen Bloodline to move through it freely but not the water beyond.

“What you all see is the Sahaelian symbol,” Lyshyla said as she came up from behind Oadira. Blood still dripped from the woman’s forehead. “If you look closely, you’ll see the eight-point star shining and giving light to the branches.”

Ozias stood in front of the Nibiru opening, looking at Nabopollassar’s seal and the open sea just beyond it. The sea tunnels were located throughout the bottom of the sea floor, allowing any Orishan to walk through Nabopollassar’s seal and be dry. The sea tunnels also prevented water from entering through the protective barrier.

“I’m going to open up Nabopollassar’s seal and flood the tunnel,” Ozias said. “It’ll take time before the water empties out after this is done.”

Lyshyla shook her head. “You’ll need to leave the barrier open for only a short time, otherwise the tunnels will completely flood with ocean water and won’t be able to drain.”

“Then I’ll do it quickly!” Ozias shouted.

“It takes two people to open Nabopollassar’s sapphire water seal. There are two key slots. You both know what needs to be done,” Lyshyla said.

Oadira and Ozias used their Orishan artes to conjure glowing blue keys to open the door to the sea.

“What’s the plan after we flood the tunnels?” Oshún asked. He stood next to his brothers, Oxum and Oya, scratched and shaking from the night’s ordeal. It had been their fault the spiders had attacked, since they had wandered off against the wishes of Lyshyla and had fallen into a Treep nest in a neighboring tunnel. Oadira was happy her sons were alright, but still frustrated with their carelessness. They were only 13, but they were princess of Sahael and needed to understand the power and importance of their lives.

“We follow the flow of the current to the northern gate of Negrallis,” Lyshyla answered. “We can reenter the tunnels from there and make it to Neir’s Realm unharmed.”

Oadira turned to the crowd behind her as thousands of people swarmed closer to the tunnel. Screams echoed from the back of the population as the spiders continued their assault.

“Orishan people!” Oadira shouted. “Remember what I said. Water is the source of our life and power. I gave all of you the ability to breath under water, so stay together in the currents. My husband, King Ozias, will open the portal slowly with my help so no one is washed away. The spiders will drown. Take courage!”

Nabopollassar’s water seal was lifted by Ozias and Oadira. Water entered the caverns slowly, preserving the integrity of the Nibiru tunnels. In a few minutes, everyone and everything was completely submerged in water. Many of the people started to panic as they held their breath and attempted to swim.

Be at peace, Oadira spoke to their minds. *You are safe. Breathe freely of the water and embrace your Orishan heritage.*

The young princes swam over to those struggling, telling them telepathically to breathe slowly and that all would be alright. Soon, everyone was moving freely, breathing underwater.

The dead bodies of Treeps large and small floated past, indicating their plan had worked. Now all they needed to so was swim out, follow the currents to the next tunnel entrance, and pray whatever water they had let into the tunnels would drain and allow them safe passage to Neir’s Realm.

The population moved through Nabopollassar’s water seal, exiting of the tunnels and exposing themselves to the open waters of Aarde. Oadira looked up at waters clear and clean, with a hint of light filtering through the ocean. She had only swum in ocean waters once before, and that was when trying to escape from slavers and colonial forces shooting arrows at her and Ozias after they jumped from the slave ships. Her powers had manifested the moment she touched the water, but as the arrows flew around her, she had no chance to savor the feeling of the ocean or the power it afforded. Now she looked around as her people floated with her, breathing of the waters that gave them life. She could stay here forever amongst the waves, free and unfettered from the world above and its troubles.

The people's cerulean eyes lit up, allowing them to witness the vastness of the marine world as if they were seeing through the eyes of the fish as they swam following the new current.

Allow the current to pull us, as Lyshyla instructed, Oadira communicated with her people. Many nodded, and they allowed themselves to flow with the water in whatever direction it chose.

Ozias and Lyshyla swam next to Oadira, along with their triplet sons. *Where will the current lead us?* Ozias asked.

To the underwater caverns on the ocean floor, Lyshyla answered. It won't take us long to find them. While in Neir's Realm I memorized much of the use of the tunnels and their offshoots. We will flow for less than an hour and then the cave entrances will be easy to see.

And so, it was. Oadira and her people drifted with the currents for an hour, content and peaceful, until Ozias pointed at the sea floor beneath them.

I see the water caverns. Look!

They entered the caverns and traveled through them until they spotted additional underwater tunnels in the distance. They were dark and spacious, full of fish, lizards, and turtles.

We are safe for now, Lyshyla said. *This cavern will provide us adequate protection as we move through it methodically.*

Finally feeling safe, Oadira looked at her boys as they swatted at passing fish and smiled. *What happened in the tunnels was intense.*

It was, Oya agreed.

The children performed well, Ozias said.

And none of it would have happened had they been mature enough to listen to their king and queen, Oadira said, floating there with her hands on her hips. *When we finish this journey, there will be consequences for your foolishness.*

Yes, Mother, the boys said in unison.

Now go, Ozias waved, face less stern than Oadira would have liked. *Care for your people. Comfort them. Find out who was lost to the spiders and return with a tally. You are princes of Sahael. Go and act like it.*

Yes, Father! Oxum grinned.

The boys swam off and began telepathically communicating with the people. Lyshyla floated next to Oadira and Ozias.

Your children are growing up and maturing. Their gifts are growing. Those same gifts will help them shape Aarde for the better, benefitting Sahael, Lyshyla said.

What do you mean to shape Aarde for the better? Oadira asked.

They have ancient blood and possess the power to inspire others to do many things, Lyshyla answered.

Solomon said those same words to my sisters and I, Oadira said, feeling her long braids floating against the skin of her cheek.

Indeed. And look what you've accomplished. So many of the slaves from Lucedale and the Lalaurie estates are free because of your inspiration. The people of Iceoth have returned to the

Chosen Bloodline, and we are closer than ever to reclaiming Sahael. That is no small list of accomplishments. Lyshyla said as she turned her attention back to their surroundings. *Caverns are dotted all over the seafloor of Aarde. Nabopollassar's sapphire water seals prevent water from entering, allowing us all the time needed to travel to each of them, passing through each water seal.*

Will each seal open for us? Oadira asked.

No, most of them were sealed off after the fall of Sahael, Lyshyla answered.

What else below the surface was cut off from Sahael? Oadira asked.

According to the maps I memorized in Neir's Realm, the Sahaedron Kingdom and the underwater tribes were cut off from contact with Sahael, Sahaeland, and Sahaerion.

Sahaedron? That place sounds interesting. Ozias said, listening intently.

There is a reason for that, Lyshyla replied. *Sahaedron is the water kingdom of the Orishas located in Sahael that was created by the gods of this world, Ishtar and Obatala. It's one of four kingdoms needed to help restore Sahael. As we've known since Oadira arrived in Iceoth almost fifteen years ago, the currents are bringing the Orisha diaspora back to Sahael. Ishtar and Obatala's phrase is ringing true in the ears of the Ancient Order.*

Ishtar and Obatala's phrase? Oadira asked.

Ishtar and Obatala called the firmament Alkebulan. Ishtar and Obatala then said, 'Let the bloodlines in Sahael be gathered into one place, and let the skies of Sahaerion be united,' and it was so. Ishtar and Obatala called the dry land Sahaeland and connected it in the center of Alkebulan, where life started. Then Ishtar and Obatala lifted the underground and named it

Sahaedeath to hear the dead sing throughout all of Aarde. Then Ishtar and Obatala ordered the gatherings to occur in the seas of Sahaedron, the lands, the floating mountains, and finally the skies, where it would conclude the Signs of the Times. Only then would Aarde know it's complete. That is the Creed of the Ancient Order, written and etched into your lineage. It'll unite them all under the Sahaelian banner when recited to the people. Your children are important to Aarde.

Queen Oadira rubbed her stomach and the tiny unborn child growing slowly inside. *I'm scared of what they'll face. I grew up on an estate where mothers killed their Black babies to avoid a life of slavery. That is how they showed love and mercy by ending their lives before they started.*

It's okay, Ozias said, hugging his wife close. *You were their salvation as your mother provided salvation to you.*

Oadira floated there in the warm water of the cave, remembering the horrors of her childhood watching people suffer while she was kept safe in the manor house waiting to be sold for her breeding rights. She knew hate was not an effective emotion, and yet hate still festered in her heart.

The pure hatred of witans who would have my sons killed and enslaved due to the color of their skin makes me sick to my stomach, she spat telepathically. *My husband, children, and I are the only pure-blooded Orishan's left in Aarde. It was no mere coincidence that brought my husband and me together when we found each other. Solomon set me on this path, and his cryptic words have proven true at every turn, as has his counsel. Many years ago, Solomon ordered me to find the Orishan bloodline, knowing that it was needed to restore Sahael.*

What are you saying? Lyshyla asked.

He told me that my bloodline would supersede the patriarchal bloodline of whoever I would marry. If that man was not of ancient blood, then by right, his bloodline becomes mine, Oadira said.

Lyshyla nodded. *What you say is true. But keep in mind, it's only if the one you're marrying isn't a king. I learned much in Nier's Realm; much I still need to share with you.*

Over the next few hours, the group journeyed through the underwater cavern, catching glimpses of daylight filtering through the waters above when they came to an opening. The princes, along with other children and teenagers among the crowd, grew restless and began fooling around with the sea life in the area; playing with large jellyfish, snapping turtles, piranhas, and other dangerous creatures roaming the sea of Aarde. They forced Lyshyla and Ozias to have to chase after them as they often were separated from the group, slowing them down repeatedly.

They're scared and this is how they are expressing it, Oadira said to Ozias as he voiced his frustration.

That's evident, Ozias replied. *We'll need to keep an eye on them. They've dealt with a lot of traumas recently...all of them have. And our people will deal with even more in the coming years.*

Oadira took his hand. *The best thing to do is talk to them, listen, and ask them questions.*

I'll keep a close eye on them, Lyshyla said. *They are important to our future, and I would be derelict in my Educator duties if I let them go astray at this point. The past eight years have been long, and even if our time together as a people right now is short, know that I will never abandon those boys.*

Thank you, Oadira smiled.

They fear they're going to lose their parents like you two have, Lyshyla said.

That won't happen, Ozias stated firmly. She pondered Lyshyla's words for a moment. What did she mean when she said their time together as a people right now may be short? Just as she reached out with her mind to ask Lyshyla the question, her sons approached.

Are we there yet? Oya asked as he swam toward his parents and Lyshyla.

No, Lyshyla confirmed with a sad expression. *But when we arrive, everyone will have to be on their guard. Also, it will be time for us to part ways.*

Wait! Why? Oadira asked.

The six of you, and myself as an Educator, are the only ones who can pass through the Negralli gate, Lyshyla confirmed. *Ossa will take the rest of the Orishan people and travel by the ocean floor until we arrive in Sahael. Ossa will lead them.*

But they can't enter the nation without the Nairohenge gates, Ozias said, confusion on his face. *How will Ossa get into Sahael? He's not of ancient blood. The gates will not allow him to pass.*

Lyshyla nodded, long braided hair wafting around her head in the water. *No, but he can arrive on the continent with the Orishan people and wait behind the walls for your arrival. Ossa will lead the people to Sahael. I've already spoken with him regarding this eventuality as we have traveled through the tunnels over the last few days. I have given him a map that, once it is time for us to spit off, he will know where to lead the people.*

Why didn't you tell us this before we left the pyramid on Iceoth? Oadira asked. Lyshyla had always shared information when it was needed, but Oadira tired of half answers. Eight years in Neir's Realm had not changed the woman one bit.

Because you would not have gone, Lyshyla answered. *You would not have left your people unless you were in a position where you had no other choice. Only those of pure blood can enter*

Neir's Realm without the knowledge of an Educator. I am sorry. Now, there is an outpost a day's journey from here once we renter the tunnels. Ossa and the people can resupply there if needed since much of the gear was left behind as we escaped the Treeps.

So, you can come to Nier's Realm with us, but no one else can. Oadira stated.

Yes, Lyshyla said.

Will you be permitted past the Negralli gates at the entrance to Nier's Realm? Ozias asked.

Yes. As an Educator who studied at Timbuktu, I know the knowledge necessary to traverse the barrier.

After finding the next entrance to the Nibiru Tunnels, the population passed through the barrier and breathed air once more. After a day's journey they came upon a small settlement in the caves where travelers were welcomed and the Orishans ate and slept soundly for the first time since encountering the Treeps.

Over the next two days, their journey continued. Oadira avoided Lyshyla out of anger and frustration. She had no desire to leave her people as she and her family searched for information on how to use the Nairohenge Gates. The more she thought about it, the angrier she became. Lyshyla had spent eight years in Nier's Realm. She could have given them whatever knowledge she had, but as always, the Educator shared only what was needed in the moment. On top of everything, symptoms of morning sickness had begun to manifest, forcing Oadira to throw up on occasion as they walked through the dark tunnels.

"We'll soon be outside of the Negralli gates," Lyshyla told Oadira on the third day from the settlement. "It's time to gather the people and let them know we will be separating soon."

Oadira gathered her people and addressed them.

"The blood running through your veins has been made pure

through Nile's flame, enabling each of you the ability to use the power that we wield in a small capacity. Per my orders, Lyshyla is to stay with the royal family. As you all travel to our ancestral home of Sahael, led by Ossa, you will be the only ones on the continent. While you won't be able to enter the sacred center of Sahael, you will be able to settle the lands around the great walls. Rebuilding will be your primary objective. Claim for yourselves every single right that belongs to you.

"The battle we wage is not for ourselves alone but for all Sahaelians. It's a fight never before witnessed. In the Age of Enlightenment, witans have threatened to adopt such a cowardly creed in the treatment of Black people born and bred on their soil. They've stripped us of verbiage and subterfuge, and in its naked nastiness, the new Narsan creed says: 'Fear to let Black people even try to rise, lest they become the equals of the witans.' And this is the land that follows the precepts of White Darkness that has slowly entered and taken over the witans' red hearts.

"I leave you all in the capable hands of Mansa Ossa Musa, our most trusted general, and lifelong friend of King Ozias. He will lead you all to Sahael. The Orisha bloodline blesses you all with eternal life, enabling you everlasting youth. Armed with this knowledge, I order you to use it to go forth and help renew and restore our people."

The people cheered and cried, clapped and sang. Over the next few hours, they began to depart from the cavern, making their way toward Sahael.

Ossa approached Oadira and Ozias, hugging each of the princes. "My friends, it is with heavy heart that I lead our people to their homeland."

"They are in good hands," Ozias said, eyes brimming with tears.

"Keep them safe," Oadira said as she embraced Ossa.

"I will, my queen," he replied. "And when the time comes for us to enter the sacred center of Sahael, your people will be ready for you."

CHAPTER II

AN ANCIENT ULTIMATUM

Nier's Realm, Nieth City

The royal family traveled to the entrance of Nier's Realm, walking and swimming along the cavern floor and exposing themselves to the water mountains surrounding the entrance.

"Father, look!" Oya said.

"What is it?" Oadira asked.

"There are dark holes appearing under us as we walk up the water mountains," Oxum said.

"I see them also," Lyshyla said, pointing them out to Ozias and Oadira.

"We're going to follow them up the water mountain," Lyshyla said.

To have better visibility, the royal family blinked their eyes twice, activating their Orishan gifts. Their tattoos lit up, and their eyes went from sapphire to cerulean. One of the dark holes activated, causing them to be sucked into it as they traveled up the water mountain.

Beathe of the water! Oadira shouted telepathically. *The current is too strong to fight! Stay together!*

While falling, Oadira observed specks of kyanite in the water, matching the color of their eyes. They acted like enhancers, strengthening their powers and allowing them sight to see through the void of dark water and space at long distances. Seemingly from out of nowhere, they noticed five or six lights that began to appear on the inner walls within the dark-blue area. They stood around the circumference of the space, falling through the emptiness.

Oadira looked around, feeling weightless with nothing to grab hold of.

Is this a trap? she asked. *What are we to do?*

Keep falling? Ozias said.

I don't know but figuring this out is our main priority right now, Oadira said.

There must be a way through this dark space if we're to get to Nier's realm and the Negralli gates, Ozias said. *How do we enter or move in the emptiness of this dark-blue space?*

This is the Nibiru space, Lyshyla answered. *All the bright Kyanite colors are coming from within it.*

The light began to emanate more fiercely and pulsate from the cerulean specks that surrounded them in the water. They traveled farther and deeper inside of the dark emptiness, pulled along by the current. The cerulean light began to grow dimmer and dimmer behind them. They had reached the bottom when suddenly the water began to drain until the stood all alone on a dark Orichalcum platform with a symbol on it. Once the water had completely drained, Oadira focused on the symbol beneath them in the dark metal.

"What is this?" she asked.

"We're standing on the Orishan symbol of Odunde on the base of the Marula Tree with branches coming out of it," Lyshyla said. "This is the entrance to the gateway to Neir's Realm. What we encountered above is merely a distraction for those seeking the entrance, but not of the bloodline. When I arrived here years ago, it took me time to realize that I had been taught about the hidden entrance while studying in Timbuktu. Below the symbol is the entrance to the Nairohenge Gates."

"Only one of the branches was lighting up," Ozias said.

"Why is that?" Oadira asked.

"Only one branch was in sapphire. There are also six sets of footprints below it," said Lyshyla, pointing them out.

"What is this?" Oadira asked.

"This Orichalcum platform needs to be activated by the blood of the ancients," Lyshyla said.

"What does this symbol of the Marula Tree mean with the branches coming out of it?" Ozias asked.

"Well, it would seem that placing your feet on these sets of footprints will activate the Marula Tree and one of the four branches," Lyshyla said.

"But we are missing one set of footprints," Oadira said, who brought this to the attention of Lyshyla. Lyshyla looked at Oadira's belly and then made eye contact with her.

"Oadira, you're pregnant, thus when the time arrives and the child comes of age, the other set of footprints will light up," Lyshyla said.

"I understand," Oadira acknowledged.

Ozias, Oadira, Oshún, Oxum, and Oya placed each of their feet in the footprints on the engraved foot images. When they did, the symbol of the Marula Tree lit up, causing the platform to push them up toward the inner surface where water magically held itself suspended in the air several thousand feet above. As the platform moved upward, spinning slowly in a circular, clockwise motion, the kyanite particles started to form around their torsos, legs, and arms.

"What's happening? Oadira asked.

"The Power of the Ancients has recognized your presence, anointing your family as the rulers of this realm, for reasons beyond my understanding. Nier's kyanite particles are enhancing your Orishan gifts while adding armor to your body's abilities, artes, and powers," Lyshyla said.

The moving platform reached the inner surface, splashing through the suspended water and revealing the royal family in all their glory to Nier's realm as they stood proudly on the platform. Their eyes glowed cerulean.

Their natural blood lineage of tattoos shone the same color as their eyes. They were each cloaked in ancient armor, and each of the young boys held double-sided axes, Kandu swords, long swords, and daggers.

The moment they stepped off the platform, the Negralli gates appeared in the distance though a thick mist. The shadows of warriors in thick Sahaelian armor could be seen all around them, obscured by the fog, but obvious.

"We made it!" Oshún said, taking a deep sigh of joy.

"The Negralli gates are before us," Lyshyla said.

"Everything is lighting, I can't see! There is smoke everywhere," Oadira said.

"Just be patient, the smoke will subside," Lyshyla said.

"We are surrounded by thousands of Negralli knights," Ozias said.

"It's okay. Their sole purpose was to protect the Nier's realm at all costs," Lyshyla replied. She turned to the knights all around them. "Behold, as promised! I have brought the last pure bloodline of the Orishans! Behold and rejoice!"

The Negralli knights immediately fell to one knee, chanting *"Chukwu"* multiple times. The then formed two lines in front of the family, with a space to walk in the middle.

"They're forming a line," Oxum said.

"It's a path leading to the Negralli gates. Follow it," Lyshyla suggested. "The Negralli knights are going to escort us from here."

The family followed Lyshyla along the line of knights until they came to a circular portal at the end of a long stone chamber.

"Enter in, members of the Chosen Bloodline," Lyshyla smiled.

Oadira walked through first, feeling her skin tingle as she passed into Nier's Realm. The air smelled of smoke and the vapor they had witnessed on the other side of the entrance persisted.

Ozias, Oadira, Oshún, Oxum, and Oya walked down a long stone hallway, stepping out into the sunlight of a warm day. Surprisingly, Oadira looked out on a realm in ruins and rubble, filled with smoke everywhere. The people were cleaning up the streets, and debris as if they had recently been attacked.

"What happened here?" Oadira asked.

"You will find out soon enough," Lyshyla said. "Follow me. There are many people who wish to meet you."

They were received by Emperor Olokun and Empress Yemoja. The two of them were perfect deities with unblemished Black skin. They were the stewards of the kingdom. Their bodies were well defined, full of beauty beyond measure to the naked eye.

Yemoja stood six-feet, eight-inches tall. She had long, beautiful hair down to the middle of her back and ivory teeth. Olokun stood seven feet tall and had no hair, with robes of gold and crimson. Olokun and Yemoja's eyes were as cerulean as the royal family's.

They both sat on the water thrones of Nier, motioning for the royal family to approach. On each side of the room were large statues of the previous empresses and emperors. Nieth Palace was made of ivory, Orichalcum, and sapphire stone; the floors covered in square tiles.

Oadira and Ozias knelt before the deities. Lyshyla and the boys did the same before standing again in unison.

Emperor Olokun and Empress Yemoja received them into their presence, embracing Oadira, Ozias, Oshún, Oxum, and Oya one by one.

"We thank you for making the long trip to Nier's realm," Empress Yemoja said excitedly as she stood up to address the royal family. "We are glad you are here. Lyshyla has told us so much about you and the goings on in Aarde. We are pleased you are here before us."

"The Signs of the Times are upon us," Emperor Olokun said. He nodded his head and then made eye contact with the royal family and then with Yemoja. "Your family may enter through the sub-gates, but you're not permitted beyond the Negralli gates. You're expecting a child, and entry beyond these gates is forbidden until your child is born."

"So, you know I'm pregnant?" Oadira asked.

"Our eyes tell us more than most," the empress smiled.

Emperor Olokun nodded in agreement. "Your arrival is timely. Empress Yemoja and I could feel your presence as the currents forced you to leave Iceoth. When Lyshyla informed us several months ago that she felt compelled to return to Iceoth, and that the time of your arrival had come, we were very excited, as were our people. They want to meet you very much. They are gathered in our center square now, the heart of our city and realm, to greet you."

"Thank you for welcoming us as guests," Lyshyla bowed.

"You are more than a guest, Sister Lyshyla," Empress Yemoja grinned. "You have been a friend and confidant for many years. We are glad you have returned."

"Your majesties," Ozias said, stepping forward. "This realm looks like it is rebuilding from something that happened not long ago. When we first arrived, it looked as if they were cleaning up the city from a recent skirmish."

Emperor Olokun nodded and rubbed his leg. "It was not from a battle, but rather the shifting of the earth beneath us. Earthquakes have never bothered this realm before, but over the last few years, they have become more common. We suffered one mere hours ago, before your arrival."

"We are sorry to hear that," Oadira said. "Is there anything we can do to help?"

"Yes, and no," the emperor replied.

"Oadira, you have ushered in these changes, starting with the waters that have led to the events that have taken place in Nier's realm," Empress Yemoja said. "The reversal of the currents has caused destruction all over the open waters and throughout Aarde. Typhoons, tsunamis, and whirlpools have been seen all over the oceans of Aarde. They are causing untold amounts of destruction and death to all continents. The death toll is rising every second."

Oadira had long ago become accustomed to this kind of talk. It was her fault, all the death and destruction. All because of her existence. She grew tired of it.

As if understanding her thoughts, Emperor Olokun raised the palm of his hand. "Do not misunderstand. All of this is because of you and the Signs of the Times, but none of it is your fault. Your presence has awakened and caused the submerged lands of the Sahaedron realm and the caverns to shift. Everyone is starting to feel quakes, hurricanes, and tornadoes throughout Aarde. These events are changing Aarde, and they will continue to happen until the Times are completed."

"Why are these events causing this type of destruction? How do I get them to stop?" Oadira asked.

"The sooner the Ancient Blood returns to Sahael, the sooner these catastrophes across Aarde will stop," Empress Yemoja said, letting out a light sigh of relief.

"Now is not the time to fret over such things," the emperor said as he stood from his throne. "Now is a time of celebration."

"Please follow us," Empress Yemoja said. She and Emperor Olokun led them down the royal ivory halls of Nieth. Every surface, from the walls to the pillars to the ceilings, appeared to be carved with figures and creatures in gleaming white. Oadira had never seen anything like it; never imagined anything like it. What few memories she had of her childhood in Sahael's Khartoum Palace seemed too good to be true in their opulence, but here in the palace of Nier, she realized her memories were far more than fantasy.

The royal family was escorted to the secondary rooms in Nier's realm in the sub-halls of Nieth. They remained under heavy guard as the people waited with anticipation and excitement from the center of the city. Emperor Olokun and Empress Yemoja accompanied them to the royal guest quarters consisting of many rooms.

"Thank you," Ozias said. "This is beyond any welcome we expected. Our travels have been long and difficult."

"Lyshyla never told you what to expect?" Emperor Olokun smiled, glancing at Lyshyla. "I am not surprised. Educators are not known to give information that is not first requested with a very specific question."

Oadira laughed. Apparently, the emperor felt the same way about Educators as she did.

After a brief tour, the emperors escorted the royal family to a balcony overlooking a square filled with thousands of people. Everyone cheered and waved colored flags. In the center of the square stood a series of large stone pillars, some standing tall, others laid across the tops like doorways.

The Nairohenge Gates.

"Behold!" Emperor Olokun shouted to the masses below. "I present King Ozias Ocnus and Queen Oadira Ocnus of the Orisha, their sons and Educator Lyshyla! Let them be welcome. Let them be blessed. Let them reclaim their homeland!"

Another cheer reached Oadira's ears, and she felt the emotion of the crowd. Their love for these strangers was pure. They would serve her family faithfully forever if needed. For a moment she wondered if they could stay here in this peaceful and loving place and forsake Sahael, but she knew instantly that wasn't her path, or that of her family.

After a banquet and many festivities, Oadira and her family were led back to their regal quarters. Upon entering her room, Oadira was quickly encircled by Negralli servants. Midwives and the finest doctors were sent to care for her and the unborn child.

That evening Lyshyla came to see them to make sure they were settled, and Oadira decided now was the time for a few answers.

"When the emperor took us to the courtyard at the center of Nieth, I noticed the Nairohenge Gates."

"Those were not the Nairohenge Gates," Lyshyla said. "As I told you when we stood on the barrier beneath the water chamber, the gates can only be opened by the sets of footprints. What you saw today was the Nairostone Gates. The Nairostone Gates were created by each of the realms to help large groups of people transport to each of the four realms. Each Nairostone Gate still needs a Navigator and a Medjay Gate Guardian to help them travel safely."

"Why are the Nairohenge Gates locked in the ground?" Oadira asked "How many are there exactly? As we walked through Nieth, I saw some lights in the middle of the stones that appeared to be gates as well."

"There are nineteen gates in total, with four single gates in the center. The four middle gates are shared by the four realms, Sahael, Horn, and Egyptus," Lyshyla answered. "Only the Nairohenge Gates can access Sahael, and we won't be able to activate them until your unborn child is of age."

Months passed and Oadira barely noticed the flowing of time. Everything from the food to the water itself was perfect. The royal guest quarters consisted of elaborate rooms and servants' quarters for everyone and the kids. The boys enjoyed using the inside pool in their quarters and had made friends with the children of the palace staff, as well as the training guards of the court. The thought of returning to Aarde made Oadira almost smirk, and she understood why Lyshyla had remained here for eight full years.

Several earthquakes had shaken the realm during their time, reminding Oadira that they would need to return to Sahael if they wanted the world to quiet itself and be at peace.

"We've been in these royal guest quarters for a long time now," Oadira said one afternoon as she rubbed her bulging pregnant belly. "It's nice to be waited on, but not being permitted to leave the palace has been hard on everyone, especially the children."

"The accommodations have been great. All the comforts one would ever want are here," Ozias agreed. "And at least the boys have had a chance to spar with youth their own age. The guards here are skilled and have taught our sons excellent tactics that will serve them well."

One late summer afternoon Queen Oadira delivered her last son Onika, with Ozias's support, surrounded by midwives. She appreciated the difference in the customs here in Neir's Realm that allowed her husband to participate in the birth. She remembered when the triplets were born, and she had so wished Ozias could be by her side.

After the birth, Onika was visited by the Orishan spirit guardian Ibeji, who blessed the child. Oadira chewed, severing the umbilical cord, delivering the placenta, and burning it allowing its blue essence to enter Onika's body. Afterwards, there was no ritual of urination involving Oadira signifying that Onika would be their last child and eventual High King of Sahael, capable of using the gift of shout.

The baby started fussing, so Oadira took him from hi father's arms for his first feeding.

Over the next seven days, the royal family was left alone with their new child; Lyshyla being their only visitor during daylight hours.

On the eighth day, however, they heard a knock on the door.

A Negralli messenger entered and bowed. "The royal family has been summoned. The emperors would like to see the king and queen, as well as their four sons."

Ozias and Oadira followed the messenger into the large, majestic throne room with their family in tow. Oadira held Onika in her arms. Oshún, Oya, and Oxum were slightly behind Ozias. The water thrones sat empty, but Lyshyla approached, motioning to the statues lining the walls.

"The statues all have sapphire eyes that when lit up are cerulean like yours," she said. "I know you haven't been allowed to explore much, but this whole city is made of ivory with a slight cerulean hue in color. The streets are made of Orichalcum and crafted to look like cobblestone."

"We were summoned," Ozias said, motioning his head toward the empty thrones.

"So, you have!" Emperor Olokun said loudly as he and the empress entered from the other side of the hall. "You'll excuse our tardiness. We were finishing a discussion with our captain of the guard."

At that moment a legion of warriors marched into the throne room and stood along the walls. They were dressed in exquisite armor accented with a light-cerulean cloth. The letter "N" etched on their breastplates pulsated, giving the knights great power. The knights stood side by side with the ancient family.

Lyshyla and the princes knelt on one knee, bowing their heads before the emperor and empress as Oadira bowed forward with Onika close to her chest.

"Thank you for the hospitality you've shown us the past several months," Ozias said. "We're most grateful, and we are thankful for your midwives, doctors, and nurses attending to my wife and family's needs."

Olokun nodded his head and lifted his hand with his palm up, signaling that the family should rise to their feet. They all stood and made eye contact with the two leaders.

"The times are upon us," Empress Yemoja said as she and the emperor took their seats on the water thrones.

"Time isn't on your side," Emperor Olokun agreed. "As the gods of the underwater realm, it is our place to inform you, Queen Oadira, of knowledge that has been lost; knowledge not even Educator Lyshyla had prior to her time here with us. May we speak freely to you and your family?"

"Of course," Oadira replied. The thought of learning more excited her.

Emperor Olokun nodded. "Your father, Ninqi, of the Nephilim bloodline and your mother, Nergal, of the Negralli bloodline married. They made the decision to live in Sahael many years ago while in Timbuktu. Their presence helped unite and tie this realm to Sahael."

"They married in secret to unite Nier's realm and Sahael with their unarranged marriage," Yemoja said. "That's why they went to Sahael: to help restore and tie the realms in Aarde to the homeland."

"What about the other realms?" Oadira asked.

"The three other realms that followed your parents' example of marrying in secret helped tie the other three realms back to Sahael," Empress Yemoja continued. "Those realms were Neros's realm, Nethal's realm, and Naharis's realm. They all chose to make Sahael their home to unite the four realms to preserve the Ancient Bloodlines. Nier's realm formed the Orishan bloodline, and the three other realms formed the other three Ancient Bloodlines to reside in Sahael."

Emperor Olokun interjected, "Your mother and father married and had a child through the blessings of Ibeji, a baby girl. That baby girl was you. The other three realms were blessed with three baby girls through the blessings of Ibeji as well. This helped the realms unite new bloodlines. After the four of you were born, the gates were revealed, providing the Chosen and the Ancient Bloodlines in Sahael the ability to travel all over Aarde."

Ozias looked around. "Do you think that these marriages are all linked to the events happening all over Aarde?"

"Yes," Yemoja confirmed. "The marriages are linked, but we have no other knowledge of how. If you want to find out, Sahael is where you'll find answers to your questions."

"Empress," Oadira said, stepping forward while bouncing her newborn in her arms. "If I may ask, who are the other bloodlines in the other realms? Did they have expectations required of them?"

"They each had expectations required of them. The four baby girls were to be used to unite the four realms, bringing them all to Sahael. They were responsible for starting the first gathering of the twelve tribes of Sahael when you all turned eighteen years old."

"The gathering was to be triggered by Nier's realm, home of the Negralli," Emperor Olokun said. "Then Neros's realm, home of the Negrunde; then Nethal's realm, home of the Negraté; and lastly Naharis's realm, home of the Demirrians. The four emperors and empresses were to offer guidance and direction to the new bloodlines in Sahael and in turn they would help protect and free the Alkebulan people and watch over Aarde. The Negralli, the Negraté, the Negrunde, and the Demir chose to follow Nairobi laws. The laws were a set of rules and principles used to govern everyone in Sahael and in the realms. The laws allowed all four realms equal access to Sahael to serve the Alkebulan people."

Empress Yemoja and Emperor Olokun ordered their servants to bring chairs so that the royal family could sit down and listen to them speak.

"Equal access to Sahael?" Oadira asked. "What does that mean? I thought every bloodline could access Sahael."

"Equal access meant balance would be established

throughout Aarde," Empress Yemoja informed. "With all four realms protecting and using their gifts and talents to serve the Alkebulan people. Sahael was to maintain that balance as the central power in Alkebulan. These were the terms set by the four realms known as the law until the Narsans disrupted that delicate balance of peace in Aarde."

"I've heard of the Narsans my entire life," Oadira said with bite to her words. "All I know is that they serve Natas, but even the archives in Iceoth said very little about them. Please, give me the knowledge I need."

A smile filled Emperor Olokun's face. "You are a righteous daughter of Sahael, Oadira. You shall be given what you seek. The Narsan are a nation full of xenophobes, people who are fearful of anyone different than they are; those who don't look like them from foreign origins and nations. They're looking to assert themselves as the main superpower in Aarde. The Narsans have established witan supremacy in western Aarde and are now looking to do the same in eastern Aarde. They have perverted the four Ls—Love, Light, Life, and Luck—into their own form of dogma, turning it into a message of hate to advance their own racist agenda. The Narsans instituted slavery in western Aarde and are looking to systematically eradicate those with Black skin in eastern Aarde. The Narsans want to control Sahael, Alkebulan, Horn, and Egyptus, to control all of Aarde, and to eradicate all of the Black people."

"But first, we must get to Sahael and return the realms to balance before you turn your attention to them," Lyshyla said. "And that can't be done until the moment is right. I stayed here in Nier's Realm because I knew that time still needed to pass before Sahael could be reclaimed…and it still needs to pass further even now."

"More time?" Oadira questioned. "More time? It's been a

decade and a half…more than that, since all of this started with Solomon's council to me and my sisters at the Royal Rumble. And you're saying there is more waiting to do?"

"Yes," Lyshyla nodded.

"Were the four realms truly ever at peace with each other?" Ozias asked. "Let's be honest; everyone talks about Sahael as this amazing place of wonder and enchantment, but my ancestors left for a reason. It seems like the Chosen Bloodlines were no better than the witans in their infighting."

"You speak wisely, King Ozias," Emperor Olokun agreed. "No, they never had the opportunity to establish peace for the greater good of Sahael. The four princesses were to remedy that by creating and establishing strong bonds of friendship. With that said, the gathering never took place because of Natas's invasion."

"Why is that?" Oadira asked.

Yemoja stood up from her water throne and started walking down the steps. "Please, bring a table, so the royal family can eat."

Several guards rushed out and brought a table and chairs, followed swiftly by other servants carrying platters of fresh vegetables and steaming meats.

Emperor Olokun stepped down as well, he and his wife taking seats at the head of the table. "Discussions are always better with a good meal. Now, Queen Oadira. You asked why the invasion thwarted the gathering of the bloodlines. Well, it's simple. The Narsans killed every member of the royal families inside of the palace. It was all done to retrieve Nzingha's obsidian key, buried in Necrosis's chamber deep in the royal crypt."

"What did they want with Nzingha's obsidian key?" Oadira asked.

"Only the Demirrians can answer that," Emperor Olokun said.

"Then why keep Nzingha's obsidian key around the dead in the first place?" Oadira asked.

Empress Yemoja took a bite of bread and nodded toward Oadira. "When royal family members die, their essence enters the obsidian key to keep the souls and the power of the dead from traveling to Naharis's realm through Nabopollassar's seal, passing Nebuchadnezzar's Portal. This gives Naharis's realm the power and ability to unbind all things to death. The taking of Nzingha's obsidian key has forced Naharis's realm out of balance with the other three realms. They immediately declared war on the three realms after the retrieval of Nzingha's obsidian key."

"The other realms?" Oadira asked.

"Emperor Olokun and I don't know how the other realms fared. As far as this realm, the Ennead invaded, killing as many as they could," Empress Yemoja said. "The Narsans followed. The Ennead invaded Nier's realm with Captain Lynch who demanded Nzingha's sapphire key."

Ozias coughed, as if her words disturbed him. "So, let me get this straight. The Ennead invade Khartoum Palace to retake Nzingha's obsidian key, which got placed in the ground in Necrosis's chamber. Then this Captain Lynch shows up with the Ennead and asks for Nzingha's sapphire key?"

Olokun nodded his head in agreement.

"Now you are saying that another key of Nzingha's, this one sapphire, used to be in Nier's realm and it is now gone?" Ozias asked.

"Yes," Emperor Olokun said.

"That's a lot of keys," Oya mumbled as he chewed a piece of succulent meat.

"Hush, son," Oadira chided as Onika began to fuss in her arms a bit.

"I'm just saying," Oya shrugged, "there's lots of keys and lots of gates and lots of people who want to kill us. We run from our homes again and again and again, and each time someone tells us there's somewhere else to go, or something else to find, or some other sacrifice we have to make." He stood, voice rising in volume. "I'm sick of it! Why can't anyone just tell us how we can get home and live in peace. All I want to do is study my insects and learn about the natural world, not fight and kill and find out we have ten other stupid things to find."

Ozias stood as well, anger in his eyes at his son's disrespect. But before he could speak, Oadira grabbed his arm.

"I understand Ossa's frustration," she said in a calm voice. "Though I disagree with his tone. Solomon only gave me part of the answers I sought. Lyshyla and the archives gave me a few more crumbs, and now you're dumping even more on us. The forces allied against us are a legion of legions, all lead by a demon made flesh. Beyond that, we have the threat of the Ukáváál who destroyed our ancestor's world. Now, all I want to know is how do we get back to Sahael and destroy everyone who would hunt us to extinction."

Oya sat back down. His brothers looked at him in awe, as if only he had the courage to voice their shared thoughts. They looked at their mother with even more awe for backing him up. The emperor and empress looked at each other.

Yemoja breathed deeply. "I understand your frustration, but defeating evil such as Natas, the Ennead, the Narsan, the Ukáváál, even the witans of the colonies, is not so easily accomplished. Knowledge is truly your best weapon, and we will give you everything we can."

"Fine," Oadira said as she flicked her finger against her fork. "Why is Nzingha's sapphire key so important?"

"Without Nzingha's sapphire key in Nier's realm, there is

no way magic can disperse from Nullify's Gate providing magic to Nier's realm," Emperor Olokun confessed. "It hinders Nier's realm and the ability to control all life below the waters of Aarde. The stewards of this sphere refused to hand over Nzingha's sapphire key, so Captain Lynch ordered First Commander Shu of the Ennead Legion to kill every Negralli person in the city."

"So, they let the people die?" Ozias asked.

Emperor Olokun nodded his head once more. "A deal was reached to protect the remaining civilians."

"What did they agree to?" Oadira asked.

"The slaughter of the Negralli people forced the stewards to give up Nzingha's sapphire key to prevent more deaths," Emperor Olokun said. "They wanted to preserve the remaining lives inside Nier's realm, so a deal had to be struck. Your grandmother and grandfather, Oadira, offered up Nzingha's sapphire key to save Nier's realm, the city of Nieth, and the Negralli people. After getting what they wanted, the Ennead looked to destroy the Nairohenge Gates in this realm. Luckily, the gates had retracted into the ground the moment Nier's realm was breached by Captain Lynch and the Ennead."

"So, my grandparents gave up Nzingha's sapphire key?" Oadira asked, surprised. She had never heard anything about her grandparents, let alone the fact they handed a powerful ancient artifact to evil men.

Empress Yemoja took a drink of wine and looked at Oadira. "They were able to make the agreement to save the Negralli people. Yemoja and I were summoned to Nier's realm until Nygaard's prophecy was complete. That is how we became rulers here in this lower sphere."

"As deities of the deep-water world," Emperor Olokun continued, "we are forbidden to interfere in Aarde's affairs and the affairs regarding even this transitory realm. That is why we are telling you this. The Okavango Heart is needed if you want permanent entry into Nier's realm. According to prophecy, the Heart is made up of eight stones that are integral to the survival of Sahael and all of Aarde. Only a queen of Sahael can use it. If it's retrieved, you can save the Negralli people, Sahael, and Aarde, to fulfill Nygaard's prophecy. The gates will then open at your command, and you can enter Sahael as its rightful sovereigns."

"So, we have to find this heart thing?" Oxum asked, seemingly gaining courage from his brother's earlier outburst.

"Yes, young prince." Empress Yemoja looked at Oadira. "Or your mother will, in any case. You have a beautiful family, Queen Oadira. You were blessed with the births of perfect princes and married a wonderful king through the blessings of Ibeji. Leaving them behind will be difficult, but they'll be counting on you to free us all, so your bloodline can take on the responsibilities of Nier's realm."

"We desperately need to regain control of the seas," Emperor Olokun said bluntly. "This quest, Oadira, is Nier's only hope to restore life and vitality to the waters of Aarde."

Empress Yemoja agreed. "The Nairobi laws forbid us from bringing anyone else into this conflict. The other nations must find out on their own and act on their own accord."

"This royal family is supposed to intervene, but we are at our wits' end," Emperor Olokun said. "We're going to have to break the rules of realm law to assist them, and as deities, we can't do that."

Oadira's gaze shifted to Ozias, Lyshyla, and her four children. These demi-god rulers were asking her to travel and find an unknown artifact so she could save a people that weren't hers, all so she could one day set foot in a land that would allow freedom for all people. No joy entered her heart. She had no desire to fight for anyone else, not with her seven-day-old child nestled in her arms.

But looking at that infant, Oadira knew she had been called to bigger trials than others would be asked to bear. Would she shirk them for her own comforts? No, she would not. Such was the power of her bloodline. Still, the desire to remain at peace almost overwhelmed her. Forget about the earthquakes and the slaves and the damned prophesies. Sit back and enjoy a well-earned moment of quiet.

"What the empress and emperor are asking for isn't going to be easy," she said after a long pause. "Regardless of what they're expecting of me, the decision to embark on this mission will not be rushed. I know what I must do, but I fear I lack the will to do it." She looked down at her fourteen-year-old sons who barely understand the magnitude of the situation before them.

"I agree," Ozias said, taking her hand. "But the decision isn't yours to make alone. I will not leave you under any circumstances, and neither will my sons. If you choose to stay here forever, then we will stay. If you choose to go in search of the artifacts the emperor and empress seek, we will travel by your side, I will follow you to the end of the Aarde."

Oadira's heart swelled, Her sons nodded in agreement with their father. They truly would follow her to the underworld and back.

"Your majesties," Oadira began. "My family and I will go and retrieve the Okavango Heart. We agree to your terms and conditions."

Empress Yemoja shook her head, lips pulled down in a frown. "You're mistaken, Queen Oadira. This task is to be given to you alone. The quest is to be performed solely by the Orishan Queen of Sahael, known as the Black Madonna."

"Though it saddens me to ask, do you accept these terms?" Emperor Olokun questioned.

The joy that a moment before had filled her heart, now crashed down around her. More sacrifice! More death! More loss! And yet, her heart swelled, knowing her family would be safe, and she would see them again.

"I accept," Queen Oadira replied without looking down at her newborn son. "What will I have to do?"

The emperors breathed a sigh of relief. "We understand what we are asking of you, Queen Oadira," Yemoja said. "Your family will stay in Nieth under the Negralli knights' protection. Your belongings will be taken to the royal quarters when you are ready to set out. Take all the time you need to prepare. And as far as what you will need to do once you enter the sacred monument…we do not know. Such things are for the chosen servant to discover. We will not be able to aid you."

CHAPTER III

WATCHERS OF THE EASTERN REALM

Eastern Aarde, Nier's Realm,

The royal family was escorted and granted access to all of Nier's realm. Over the next few days, they wandered through the city of Nieth and the surrounding hillsides where wild flowers of red and gold bloomed in the autumn sun. Every evening, Oadira and Ozias would meet with the rulers to prepare for her departure and discuss news from Aarde.

During their time in the city, the royal family became more comfortable, traveling throughout Nieth and reading hieroglyphs all over the central square's walls depicting the images of their histories. Lyshyla joined them and would give tidbits of antiquity here and there, as she was wont to do. Today however, it was Oshún who seemed to be the expert on the carvings of Nieth.

"These images tell a story about how Nier was created and shaped in the water mountains in his own image," Oshún explained as the family walked through the square. Onlookers pointed and waved at the royals, young children occasionally running up and handing Oadira a flower or other trinket.

"Elbrach, one of commander Ezekiel's daughters taught me about it the other day," Oshún continued. "After Nyathera's asteroid hit in the center of Alkebulan, the first of the four Old's, Nier, immediately traveled north. The other three Olds traveled elsewhere: Neros to the east, Naharis to the south, and Nethal to the west. They were ordered by Kainoa and Kaimana to create the realms and the connection to Andalusia to help bless the Alkebulans, Hornans, Sahaelians, and the Egyptians."

"Did Elbrach try to kiss you while she was teaching this stuff?" Oya teased.

"Shut up!" Oshún replied, swinging at his brother but missing.

"Let your brother talk," Oadira said as little Onika cooed in her arms. "I like to hear that you boys are learning something while we're in Nier's Realm, even if it is a young woman doing the teaching."

"Continue, Oshún," Ozias said as he waved at one of the palace guards across the square. "I'd love to learn something from someone other than your mother or Lyshyla. It's refreshing."

"I'll remember that the next time you ask me some question of antiquity or Sahaelian gates," Lyshyla chuckled with mock reproach.

"These are all images of the original Black deities of Sahael," Oxum said, pointing at the fine stone carvings along the interior walls. "The four Old's, after creating their realms, choose watchers to watch over the four dominions. And look here," Oshún pointed to a carving of a map of the world, complete with landmasses and mountain ranges. "This is a map of Aarde. It shows everything in detail on every continent, its mountains, rivers, and streams. It even shows the Nibiru wall on this side of Aarde that separates eastern Aarde from western Aarde. You can see the four realms, Alkebulan, Egyptus, Ebony, Rome, Azteca and many other floating islands along with the horn of Alkebulan. The Cendant lands and the Dent islands are over here. This map is pretty amazing. Elbrach told me it was carved over three centuries ago."

"Maybe Elbrach has a friend that can teach me all this stuff too," Oxum giggled. "But only if she's pretty."

"Shut up," Oshún repeated with a swipe at his other triplet.

"How about I take it from here," Lyshyla said as they exited the square and entered the palace once more. "There are tapestries down the main hall that share a wonderful history. Look here. This embroidery tells the tale of the four Old's choosing the four original watchers, making them a part of the Ancient Order. The four Old's, along with Kainoa and Kaimana, Ishtar and Obatala, chose the watchers, sending them down to operate their realms."

Ozias pointed to another tapestry. "I recognize this image from one of the old archive books I read years ago when you were pregnant with the boys, Oadira. The images talk about a war in Andalusia in the city of Katunkumene, the home of Ishtar and Obatala, where every spirit came from. This would be good for the boys to learn about. This information is important."

Oadira took his hands. "Perhaps you can teach them while I'm gone. It will be good for them to keep their minds occupied…and off the pretty young ladies who seem to be showing quite a bit of interest in them."

That evening the boys ran off to play in the stream with their friends, while Lyshyla, Oadira and Ozias prepared for Oadira's departure.

"Are you sure you want to do this?" Lyshyla warned.

"Yes," Oadira said. "Though '*want*' is the wrong word. I '*will*' do it because it is necessary. I trust you to watch over my boys and make sure my youngest son is taken care of."

"I will."

Ozias picked up Onika as he began to cry. "And don't forget about me. I am a king after all and can watch my own kids."

"Where are the triplets right now?" Oadira asked with a smirk.

"They're…" Ozias stuttered. "Playing with friends."

Oadira turned to Lyshyla. "As I said, Lyshyla, I trust you to watch over my family."

They laughed and talked of other goings on in the city before eventually the boys returned to the royal quarters yelling about how much fun they had in the river.

As lanterns began to be lit throughout the city, Lyshyla gathered the royal family on the balcony overlooking the city. She picked up the baby Onika and began pacing in front of them. "As Oadira prepares to leave on her quest, there is history all of you need to know. What you learn here today will get you closer to Sahael. I was here in Nier's Realm for eight years waiting for this day when you, my queen, would set out on this journey. Let me share what I have longed to share since I returned to Iceoth almost one year ago."

Oadira and her family sat quietly, eager to hear Lyshyla's tale.

"I studied the old the old texts in Nier's Realm for years, and now I share that knowledge with you. This is old history from before the foundations of Aarde were fully built. The texts speak of Andalusia and the city of Katunkumene, home of the Old Gods, where the Lusian council called a meeting in the great ethereal city of Nairobi. They summoned every Andalusian to attend and present a solution to help save the spirits of Andalusia. The Watchers, the Chosen, and the Egyptus bloodlines came together and designed a plan to liberate Aarde from all future oppression and sin. Ishtar and Obatala's three sons, Natas, Horus, and Solomon, presented themselves as the Aardian trinity to their plan for Aarde."

"Wait," Oadira interrupted. "Solomon told me he was a son of Ishtar and Obatala, but he never said the Natas was his brother, therefore making him also the son of Ishtar and Obatala!"

"This is knowledge you must now know, my queen," Lyshyla said. "Much will be difficult to hear and comprehend. Yes, Natas is a child of the gods, with the power of the seraph. Ishtar and Obatala asked who of the three they should send down to Aarde. Solomon stepped back, as he was humble and obedient, while Natas stepped forward, wanting to be sent down to Aarde and be given the opportunity and glory to help make sure all the Andalusian spirits returned to Andalusia."

"So, they had to send someone right?" Oxum asked. "Was it Natas? He destroyed Sahael!"

Lyshyla shook her head. "Horus, the youngest of the three brothers, would be sent down to Aarde to save and redeem woman and man. Solomon was happy for his younger brother. Natas, however, rather than rejoice, left the council upset, taking matters into his own hands. The council stayed in session, asking to hear Natas's plan at the request of Horus and Solomon. Natas presented a plan that had potential except for one fatal flaw. Natas wanted to take free will away from the Andalusians entering Aarde, guaranteeing Ishtar and Obatala that he wouldn't lose a single brother or sister. Natas wanted to control all four realms on Aarde, guaranteeing everyone would return to their presence. Natas rejected his parents' original plan, telling them that too many of his brothers and sisters wouldn't make it back. Insisting they didn't love all their children; Natas told the council that Ishtar and Obatala were misleading the people."

“What happened?” Oya breathed.

Oadira listened in silence, unable to comprehend that Natas, the evilest thing in existence, the beast who had destroyed her home and killed her mother, was a seraph-child of the creators. The entire city below them seemed to sit in quiet anticipation along with her as Lyshyla continued.

“Well, young Oya, the council rejected Natas’ plan. He lacked understanding that the spirits were being sent so they could be tested and prove to themselves whether or not they could become like Ishtar and Obatala, earning the right of creation.

“But the counsel’s rejection filled Natas with anger and resentment. He waged a civil war in Andalusia, recruiting Andalusian spirits to his cause. Natas filled them with lies that his own version of the better plan, the Nauthian gospel he called it, guaranteeing them all a way back to Andalusia. After many epochs, Natas had nearly one-third of the Andalusians on his side. After several more epochs, an army of bodiless hosts were cast out of Obatala and Ishtar’s presence because of their rebellion and lust for personal power. The Parental Creators sent them to the four realms of outer darkness as lost and fallen spirits, never getting the opportunity to receive a body of flesh and bones.”

“Lord Commander Natas was cast out of Andalusia and sent to the Outer Realms of Darkness to remain in isolation for all eternity?” Ozias asked.

Lyshyla handed Ozias the baby. “Yes, but as you know, he didn’t stay there. Natas escaped the Outer Realms of Darkness by his own ingenuity.”

“How did he get into Aarde?” Ozias asked.

“That knowledge has not yet been revealed, even in the libraries of Timbuktu or here in Nier’s Realm,” Lyshyla answered. “It is enough to know that Natas escaped, using his angelic body to shift between his black skinned form and a white skinned form. He sought to destroy his parents' plan, which meant destroying the spirits who rejected him, who he once claimed to love and wished to save. He became Lord Commander Natas, a blight and terror throughout Aarde.

"This forced Ishtar and Obatala to alter their plans. They sent Horus down to redeem all Aardians from their sins, giving them the opportunity to return to their presence. They knew Lord Commander Natas would enact his plan on Aarde, so they kept Horus's birth to themselves. Ishtar and Obatala, with the consent of the Old's, sent down the Watchers: the Negralli, the Negrunde, the Negraté, and the Nelio. Each were sent to the four realms to use their powers to protect Aarde from Natas. Nier's realm was inhabited by the Negralli, who were blessed with the ability to use magic. Neros's realm was inhabited by the Negrunde who were blessed with the ability to provide life, blessing Alkebulans with knowledge, strength, and memories. Nethal's realm was inhabited by the Negraté who had the power to communicate with the souls and spirits once life had been granted to an Alkebulan."

"What about Naharis's realm?" Oadira asked.

"Naharis's realm was inhabited by the Nelioan's, who were blessed with power and dominion over the dead. They were tasked with transporting in the middle of the night the bodies of the dead from any location to Naharis's realm to rest eternally after all ceremonies had been completed."

"So, all four realms were tasked with responsibilities to help see Ishtar and Obatala's plan through to the end?" King Ozias asked.

"Yes. Ishtar and Obatala sent Neolithic to create and build chambers in each of the four realms. The second thing they did was send Nullify to create gates in each of the four realms. The third thing they did was have Nebuchadnezzar create portals, allowing the four realms to be connected to Andalusia. They then charged Nabopollassar's to create four seals on Nullify's gate in each of the four realms. Ishtar and Obatala secretly arranged the four marriages of the Watchers with their four great-granddaughters, Nergal, Ninti, Morrighan, and Arishkegal. The Divine blessed Nergal with the Nephilim bloodline and betrothed her to Ninqi, ruler of the Negralli. Their two bloodlines reforged the old Orishan bloodline."

"My mother is one of the great granddaughters of the Divines?" Oshún said in shock as he heard about his parents.

"Oadira is the great-granddaughter of Ishtar and Obatala," Ozias said, bouncing his son in his arms to keep Onika from crying. He looked at his boys, sitting on the balcony next to him, eyes wide. "My sons are descended from the Divine Creators!"

"Yes'" Lyshyla smiled. "Ninti was blessed with Eloquimmian blood and betrothed and married to Enil, ruler of the Negratan realm; their bloodlines formed the Hausan bloodline. Arishkegal was blessed with Anunnaki blood and betrothed and married to Enqi, ruler of the Negrundian realm, which fused their lineages, creating the Yoruban bloodline. Their last great-granddaughter Morrighan was blessed with Nelio blood and betrothed and married to Sekhmet, the ruler of Naharis's realm. Their bloodlines fused together, forming the cursed Demirrian bloodline."

Oadira sat forward. So many questions clawed at her brain, and she felt like now she would have answers.

"Tell me about the son of Natas," she said. "the one in the cloak so dark no light can escape it. The one we say gathering the bodies with the Ennead in the forest before the old battle of Iceoth."

"Dameon is the son of Natas," Lyshyla answered. "Who Obatala and Ishtar were responsible for after casting out his father and the death of his mother, Lara, in the Andalusian civil war. They took on the responsibility of raising him and allowed Dameon to live in Andalusia. The old texts teach that one day he disappeared and has not been seen or heard since. It is said he attacks the nine divine bloodlines, tribes that were selected and ordained by the divine after the Watchers were sent down to protect the realms. The divine blessed, sanctified, and gifted four of the tribes: the Orisha, Yoruba, Hausa, and Demir. The five remaining tribes were the Horn, Egyptians, Romans, Aztecs, and Ebony. The ancient names of these eight tribes are known to us as the Oralian's, the Astorians, the Eagalians, the Lysinnians, the Nelio and lastly the Rysallians. The other two, there is no record of them. The Rysallians are the only witan tribe the divine sent down to Aarde and blessed with adaptation, echolocation, and linguistics, as were the other eight.

"The tribes that were a part of the Great Expulsion, an event that forced the remnants of the tribes out of Sahael, were targeted by Natas and Dameon. The Oralian's were led by Nygaard who at the time headed off the ice lands of Iceoth to remain isolated and protected. The Astorians chose to go to the sand lands of IFF, the deserts deep inside the island to avoid being found. The Eagalians chose their home way up in the mountainous lands of Nuberia in the west, choosing isolation for the preservation of their people. The Demirrians were enslaved and placed in the dungeons, tortured one by one in Naharis's realm. They never had the opportunity to escape. At this moment, they are lost and their whereabouts are unknown to everyone."

Lyshyla paused. "And there is one other group of people that I must tell you about…my people."

"You're of the Orishans of Iceoth like us, right?" Oxum said with a shrug.

"No, young Oxum. I am a Lysinnian. We Lysinnians

traveled to western Aarde, taking refuge in the underground stone kingdom of Inheritance that was hidden below the surface."

"A kingdom in a cave?" Oya said. "Like the tunnels we went through to get to Nier's Realm?"

Lyshyla smiled, though her face looked sad. "Much more beautiful. The Lysinnians supposedly split into three groups. One-third of their bloodline went to Egypt, another third went to the Ivory Islands, and the last third were pursued all over Aarde until they found refuge in eastern Aarde in Ivory, where they became the Moors, and Inheritance Island where they eventually became the Demir."

"You said there were nine sacred tribes, and you both have spoken about five of them but nothing about the Rysallians," King Ozias said.

"Solomon tried to help the Rysallians," Lyshyla continued. "But they refused his help, going out west to thrive on their own accord. There is a large interactive image of the Marula that covers the entire wall in the palace archives here, with the Orishan, Yoruban, Hausan, and Demirrian symbols written on the top of the Tree. The Marula Tree contains every tribe that lives in Sahael, Egyptus, Horn, and Alkebulan. There are other tribes that haven't been found yet, the Myrillians, Kaiyllians, Cycillians, and Tyrillians."

The family sat quietly, but Lyshyla simply looked out on dark the city below them. Lanterns began being blown as the hour grew late.

"We can continue this at another time," Lyshyla said. "Rest well, my royal charges. Soon you will be torn from each other for a time, but you will one day see the sunrise in Sahael and know you have brought peace to Aarde."

CHAPTER IV

KNOWLEDGE AND HISTORY

Nier's Realm, Nieth

The next day, the Nubian Guard watched over the family's every step, much to Oadira's frustration. The family was invited to dine once again with the emperor and empress, but Oadira wondered if it was considered a request or a command. The rulers of Nieth were obviously anxious for her to set out on her journey, but she still needed time with her baby. The older boys were excited to have dinner in the banquet hall, since many of their friends were children of the Nubian Guard and would be joining them for the meal and then mock battle games afterward.

Within an hour of the start of dinner, the emperor approached, smiling at Ozias and Oadira, who were watching their sons pretend to battle.

"I'd like to speak with you in private about the trials and the agreement you made prior to entering Nieth. If you all want to stay, the trials need to be completed as soon as possible if you want to get to Sahael," Emperor Olokun said.

"You said that only Oadira can complete the Watcher Trials because she is of the Chosen Bloodline," Ozias said, looking at his wife.

"Oadira is the only one here capable of completing the Watcher Trials to retrieve Okavango's heart," Olokun nodded. "I cannot stress this enough. Without the Heart, there is no redemption for Sahael, the poisoned lands of Alkebulan, or the enslaved people across Aarde. The Watcher Trials are a set of tests meant to be taken by the watcher of Nier's realm to regain control of Nier's realm and the magic that once flowed her. Once control is reestablished, balance will return to all the bodies of water in Aarde, and magic will again permeate these lands. Oadira, you will have to take the trip to Nereid's monument deep within Nier's realm."

"Emperor Olokun, do you realize that I am still recovering from my pregnancy?" Oadira asked.

The emperor shook his head. "It matters not. You will have more than enough time to recover before attempting the Watcher Trials; until that time, your family is required to stay in Nier's realm. You need to know that your youngest son must be sixteen before you can begin the Watcher Trials."

Sixteen? Oadira's forehead compressed in confusion. "what are you talking about? You made it sound like this was urgent. I've been stressed every day about leaving my children, and now you're saying I have to wait for sixteen years?!" Oadira's voice rose, drawing the attention of some of the dinner guests.

Olokun looked around and smiled at his patrons. He looked back at Oadira. "Realm law forbids it no matter the circumstances. Your youngest child must be sixteen years old. That is all I have to say on the matter for now. I hope you enjoy your dinner. We'll talk again soon."

The food and music did nothing to stem Oadira's anger. As she and Ozias walked back to their quarters, she could barely contain her frustration.

“Where’s Lyshyla?” Oadira asked as they walked past a group of guards in the main palace hallway.

“I would suspect that she is in the archives with Onika, looking for more information that may help get us to Sahael,” Ozias answered. “She wanted some time alone and asked us to join her as soon as we were able. After the Emperor’s little…announcement, I figured we should just go home and wait for the boys to return from their games, then call it a night.”

“We should join her,” Oadira said. “Empress Yemoja mentioned there’s more information about a place where all knowledge is stored in Aarde. She searches for that information, knowing it will help us get to Sahael. Let’s go now.”

Turning immediately, Oadira and Ozias descended to the lower palace levels and entered the archives, which looked surprisingly similar to the pyramid library back in Iceoth, as if the two locations had been designed by the same artifact. The only difference seemed to be that here in the city of Nieth, the archive was far more opulent and well-adorned.

Lyshyla sat at a table piled high with books in a sitting area where four different bookshelves converged. Next to her was Onika’s bassinet, where the infant slept soundly.

“What are you doing?” Oadira asked.

“Looking for a way back to Timbuktu, the center of infinite knowledge and home of the Moorish bloodline located on the island of Amit,” Lyshyla answered without looking up from her book. “During the fall of Sahael, access was lost to the island, restricting travel to Timbuktu. It’s vital that all the lineages find a way back to Timbuktu.”

“I thought that was what the Nairohenge Gates were for,” Oadira replied. “That’s why I need to go on this quest, right? So, the gates can be pulled from the ground once more and we can enter Sahael."

Lyshyla looked up from the book and sat back in her chair. "The ancient Kemites built safety mechanisms, ensuring they would preserve the Nairohenge Gates in their respective realms. If they were to rise out of the ground once more, they'd find a way to operate them, even without Navigators and Guardians."

"Where are these Navigators and Guardians?" Oadira asked.

"I don't know where they are. That's what I've been trying to learn. Some of them were killed of course when Sahael fell, but many had the means to escape and likely did. What made them so interesting was that the Navigators consisted of women with elaborate designs braided into their hair to help them navigate through the Nairohenge Gates throughout Aarde. Their detailed and intricate braids were used to help the enslaved escape."

"The Egyptians, Sahaelians, Hornans, Ebonies, Aztecans, and Alkebulans and many more braided these hairstyles into their heads days before they were ready to escape," Ozias said. "I read about such things many times. They even had paintings of examples in the archives I read. Their braids were thick and tightly braided, close to their scalps, and sometimes tied into buns on the top. There were other styles they used, such as curved braids representing roads, thick braids representing hills or landmarks as they escaped captivity. Inside of their braids, they hid gold and seeds to help them survive after they escaped. The Medjay Gate Guardians were assassins who had the responsibility of defending the Navigators, ensuring their safety at all times. The information shared with you is sacred to those of ancient blood. They are in Aarde and need to be found, if the Nairohenge Gates are to be fully operational once more."

Lyshyla turned back to her book, rubbing her hands together, scouring over the information.

"Is there a power source to activate these gates?" Oadira asked.

"The power source that activated the realm and the Nairohenge Gates was in Nzingha's sapphire key," Lyshyla said. She rubbed her eyes, covering her face, and took a deep breath. "The emperor told us that the currents have created an engine to help generate magic for a short time because of you bringing change to the waters of Aarde, Oadira. We need to find out what else is needed to restore magic back to Nier's realm permanently?"

"Oadira has to complete the Watcher Trials and retrieve the sodalite relic to help restore stability, balance, and a new power source to Nier's realm," Ozias said. "The emperor was talking about it to us earlier tonight."

"Yes, right before he told me we need to wait until Onika is sixteen years old before I can even begin the trials," Oadira spat. "Everything they implied was that this all needed to happen now. Everything was a rush and immediate. Even tonight he seemed nervous about me taking too long before saying, 'Oh, by the way, you need to wait sixteen years before you can begin."

"It's all about your perspective," Lyshyla said, raising her index finger as if accenting her point.

"What do you mean?" Ozias asked.

Lyshyla again sat back in her chair. "Both of you are still young. But you will live for many centuries. Your father, Ozias, is over 300 years old. I am far older than I look as well. Emperor Olokun and Empress Yemoja are eternal beings. Time is far different from their perspective, as it will eventually be for you as well. The rulers see things not in days and minutes, but decades and centuries. For them, sixteen years is the blink of an eye. Don't be too harsh on their perspective, as after a few centuries, you will begin to see things the same way."

Oadira grabbed her braids, rubbing each little strand and thinking to herself. She hadn't thought about that before. Time may very well change how she saw the people around her as well. What would her emotional connection be like for people that would live only a fraction of her lifespan? Would she be warm and accepting like the Emperor and his wife, or slightly colder and more unfeeling like Nilhist had been?

"While you're pondering," Lyshyla continued, "Let me tell you what you need to know about the gates and using them to enter different realms. Each of the realms and their cities are set up the same way to see who is entering and leaving their realms. If those who look like us arrive, they are greeted and welcomed to stay for as long as they choose or live among the Negralli people. They are left alone and are allowed to move freely throughout the realms."

"What happens if a witan arrives through the gates?" Ozias asked.

"They aren't allowed to move freely through any of the cities and are escorted somewhere else. The last time a witan arrived though the Nairohenge Gates, he killed and enslaved the Sahaelian and Alkebulan people. Witans aren't permitted in the four realms per realm law. It's due to their predisposition to violence and evilness to take what they can't have and appropriate what they want as a cultureless race." Lyshyla tightened her fist. "It may not always be this way, but so long as the White Darkness exists, our people will be threatened. The Nubian Guards would be the first to encounter any witans when entering any of the realms."

"What if we could activate the gates?" Oadira asked.

"Ogum's Watcher Trials would need to be completed first, as you know," Lyshyla answered. "Getting there could help you get the answers we all seek by traveling to Nereid's monument. It's why you must attempt and complete Ogum's Trials."

As they stood there in the center of the library, footsteps

approached from behind them. Oadira turned to see Emperor Olokun and Empress Yemoja approaching, along with her sons.

"King Ozias," the emperor waved. "Queen Oadira. Educator Lyshyla. We are sorry to intrude, but my wife felt we should speak with you."

"Yes," Empress Yemoja replied. "My husband may not have noticed, but I did. You, Queen Oadira, were unhappy after speaking with my husband at dinner. I know that the way we do and say things can sometimes be difficult to understand."

Oadira nodded and smiled. "Lyshyla already gave me a bit of understanding in this matter. Your understanding of time is different than mine, and I'm only now grasping that."

"I apologize for any miscommunication," Olokun said with a bow. "We are very anxious for the trials to begin, and I had not considered the fact that for you, sixteen years is a long time. For us, that is not the case. Plus, we wanted to make sure your sons made it home to you safely, though it is obvious from the mock battle in the courtyard that they can take care of themselves."

"We beat all the other kids," Oya said with a smile.

"You should have seen us, Father," Oxum gushed, tugging on Ozias' robes.

Oadira chuckled and turned back to the Rulers of Niel's Realm. "Thank you for bringing our sons to us at this late hour. Again, I understand your perspective better now, and will become used to it over time, I'm sure. I do have a question though. Why have the two of you not been able to attempt Ogum's Trials. You are powerful beings and gods. Why not attempt them yourselves?"

"According to Realm law, we're forbidden to make the attempt," Emperor Olokun said. "Only the Chosen Bloodlines can enter Nereid's monument. As stewards, we are subject to your will and required to stay in Nier's realm until Ogum's Trials are completed; in addition to the Trials being completed, you may be able to activate the Nairohenge Gates in Sahaedron once more, which I know is your primary goal."

"Completing Ogum's Trials might get you closer to the island of Amit and to the great city of Timbuktu as well," Empress Yemoja said.

Oadira walked over to the archives along the wall, seeing a large pedigree chart. She recognized it as that of the Orishan House. Onika began to fuss and Oadira bent down and pulled him from the bassinet, holding him close to her chest.

"Oshún, Oxum, and Oya, come here," Oadira said. "I want you three to understand where your bloodline came from. What you all see here is where the Oralian bloodline comes from. Our bloodline and the Negralli bloodline were blessed with the same body and size as the Nephilim. Their bloodline was superior in strength and intellect compared to any other of the tribes on Aarde," Oadira said, looking at Onika in her arms. "Oshún, please read this first section."

"They were large and muscular people. Their women all stood at six-feet, five-inches tall, and their men stood seven-feet tall. Their women came in all shades, from dark to light-skinned people." Oshún read.

"Oxum, please read the next section," Oadira said.

"They possessed the ability to swim and breathe underwater. They were blessed with eternal life to never grow old. Upon a natural death or unwanted death, a cerulean aura would encrust them and then within four days, they would rejuvenate into a younger version of themselves with the same memories, knowledge, and wisdom," Oxum read. "Wow. I didn't know that!"

"Like a caterpillar!" Oya replied excitedly.

"Oya, please read the last section," Oadira asked.

"The four Chosen Bloodlines shared these characteristics and eternal gifts. The Orishan's were blessed with sapphire eyes and the ability to see through the eyes of all living creatures below the water. They could see and hear all that they needed when they were using their Orishan gifts. Once mastered, they would then use their abilities of Hydrokinesis when they were in water, or on the surface, or in the skies, any area where there was a small water source," Oya continued.

"I'm going to read this section to everyone, so listen carefully," Oadira said. She paused for a moment, taking in the information.

"It reads that Orishan clothing in this realm and in Sahael is simple and many tribes have similar styles with their own accent color. Their linen cloth was typically white and seldom dyed another color. There was little sewing. Most of their clothing was wrapped around and held in place with a belt. The Orishan styles were generally the same for both the rich and the poor alike. Orishan men wore wrap-around skirts. The length of the skirt varied; sometimes it was short and above the knee, while other times, the skirt was longer and went near the ankles. Orishan women typically wore a long wrap-around dress that went down to their ankles. Dresses varied in style and may or may not have sleeves. Both the men and women wore lots of jewelry, including heavy bracelets, earrings, and necklaces. One popular item of jewelry was the neck collars, which were made of bright beads and jewels that were worn on special occasions. They all wore knee-high, flat, Orishan shoes and sandals."

Oadira paused and looked over the archives. "There's additional information on the other tribes in these archives, showing similar characteristics in their gifts, abilities, and cultures," she said. "These charts and pedigrees are very impressive, Empress Yemoja."

"We are very proud of them," the Empress nodded.

Lyshyla walked along the library wall, passing other tapestries with family trees and golden writing. Torches blazed brightly with unnatural white light, illuminating the area like noonday. She stopped in front of one decorative drape marked with the symbol of the Moors, her own people.

"What is it you have found?" Oadira asked.

"Come see for yourself. This says my people were the Educators of the Ancient Order, possessing the ability to teach the Navigators and the Gate Guardians how to navigate through the Nairohenge Gates. We taught them how they could reach out to Sahael, Egyptus, Horn, Ebony, Azteca, Alkebulan, and Aarde. My bloodline was responsible for educating the Sahaelians, Egyptians, Alkebulans, and all the Black inhabitants of Aarde. They were tasked with helping educate the people and the royal families, so that they would always know about their history."

Queen Oadira read beside Lyshyla, pausing for a moment on a particular line of golden text.

"Children," she said, motioning for her sons to gather beside her. "Pay attention to what I am going to read next, I want you all to hear this. *The children within Sahael were educated by traveling through the Nabtahenge Gates as well. They all made their way to the city of Timbuktu to go to school. The Nairostone Gates were also able to get them there safely to and from Timbuktu daily.*"

Emperor Olokun smiles sadly. "What a blessing that was for all people. Although magic is flowing through Nier's realm, it will soon stop flowing out from Nullify's gate. What you see happening around us is all due to your eyes having contacted the waters of Aarde. The currents flowing throughout Aarde have generated a magical engine to sustain Nier's realm for a short time, which will soon run dry,"

“When that happens,” Empress Yemoja continued. “Nier’s realm will no longer have the protections from the signs and the distractions that are happening. The typhoons, sinkholes, and tsunamis that have been happening have provided you the protection to make it to Sahael.”

“It would seem that time isn’t on our side,” Oadira said. “And yet, I have to wait 16 years before I can even start.”

“The Signs of the Times will stop, and when they do, all of the bloodlines will be exposed and vulnerable, once you all arrive in Sahael,” Empress Yemoja said. “Sixteen years is not much time, in the eternal sense of the world.”

“It is to me,” Oshún shrugged.

“It won’t always be,” the emperor confirmed.

Empress Yemoja ran her finger along one of the opulent tapestries. “You need to leave Nier’s realm, Oadira, and when you return, you’ll be our replacements after the Trials as the empress and emperor. The two of you will have to come to terms with that sooner or later.”

Oadira placed her palms on her forehead as sweat made them wet. “How do you expect us to accomplish this?” Oadira asked, making eye contact with Emperor Olokun. “How is it that Nzingha’s sapphire key is capable of so much darkness, evil, and destruction? How is it asking so much of us? We’re expected to find artifacts, lead our people, traverse Aarde, open Sahael, and rule here as well? It is too much!”

“When your grandparents handed over Nzingha’s sapphire key to save the people of Nier’s realm,” Empress Yemoja said, “there was a magical power in her key that unlocks seals. That same magical power is used to bless the realm, the sea, and the Alkebulan people—until it was handed over to Captain Lynch, who personally requested Nzingha’s sapphire key for reasons we're unaware of."

Oadira's eyes grew narrow as she tightened her lips.

"What does Captain Lynch plan to do with this key?"

"I wish I knew," Empress Yemoja said. "What I do know is that Nzingha's sapphire key has the sealing power to activate Nebuchadnezzar's portal and remove Nabopollassar's sapphire seal."

Emperor Olokun stepped next to his wife and looked up at the tapestry before them. "Nzingha's sapphire key prevents an evil power that was built up and unleashed in Andalusia, which led to civil war in which one-third of the Andalusians were cast out and sent into the Outer Realms of Darkness. It led to the descending of the Watchers here on Aarde as a direct result, to keep the people of Sahael safe so that they could serve the Alkebulans. When we were on the Lusian council, they were sent down after the ancient Kemites arrived, ensuring that Aarde and the bloodlines were protected. The divines established and created the Ancient Order with the help of the Kemites to protect and preserve the ancient lineages and the magic in Nier's realm. The four realms were to keep each other in balance throughout Aarde. There are spiritless bodies beyond the shadows of darkness looking for ways to enter Aarde from the four realms of darkness: the Void, the Hole, Oblivion, and the Nothing."

"Balance in Nier's realm needs to be restored no matter the cost. This is why you must leave for Nereid's monument. The longer Nzingha's sapphire key no longer resides in Nier's realm, the longer it will take for magic to take hold if it is restored," Empress Yemoja warned.

Lyshyla walked over to where Empress Yemoja stood "If we could get to the island of Amit, I could gather more information as to what is happening to get answers to most of our questions."

"Nier's realm must be restored before any of that can happen," Empress Yemoja said. "No boats are ready currently. They were all destroyed by Captain Lynch and the Ennead."

"Once your task is completed, we will no longer hold Nier's titles. According to realm law, his titles will fall to both of you, enabling us to return back to presiding over the waters of Aarde," Emperor Olokun said.

"They need to be free of ruling over Nier's realm," Lyshyla said, looking at Oadira. "It's your responsibility as deities and emperors to help them and Aarde. We need to prepare to save Nier's realm and return to Sahael."

"We will do everything we must," Olokun agreed. "But the journey to find Okavango's heart cannot commence until that newborn is 16 years old. It will pass like the blink of an eye."

Oadira had waited to enter Sahael for 15 years already. She hadn't seen her cousins in all that time, nor had she seen Solomon. Now she had to wait another 16 years at least. She could be a grandmother by that time.

A blink of an eye? Oadira doubted that very much.

CHAPTER V

NEREID'S MONUMENT

Nier's realm, Nambissian Sea

"It's time for you to head north," Empress Yemoja said one afternoon a few days before Onika's 16th birthday.

Oadira started fidgeting with herself, twisting her ring.

The sun shone brightly above her on this spring morning. She sat in one of the gardens surrounding the palace stitching a tapestry for her son's birthday. She could barely believe he was turning 16. She could barely believe her triplets had recently turned 30 years old. They were as strong and handsome as their father, blue tattoos and eyes glowing with power and authority. She and Ozias themselves were reaching 50, and yet they looked as young as their sons. A merchant had visited the palace a few weeks before and thought Ozias, Oadira, and the boys were all siblings as opposed to parents and children.

Life had been good in Nier's Realm over the years. Odira had longed to leave in the first few years of their exile here, but she had grown to love the culture and people, the pleasant climate, and the food. She knew Ozias missed his father and best friend Ossa, as she missed her cousins and friends from Iceoth, but life had been good here, even with the occasional earthquake that still shook the landscape.

She had almost forgotten her quest for Okavango's heart entirely.

As the Empress stood over her, shadow falling on Oadira, the realization that the time had finally arrived for her to leave her family, became all too real.

"How long will I be gone?" she asked.

"I understand your concerns. I assure you, your children will be safe," Empress Yemoja said. "they are of course the best warriors in the kingdom, so you have little to worry about. Even young Onika can handle himself life few men twice his age and experience. And of course, Ozias committed to going with you long ago, and we will honor his desire. Lyshyla has also requested to journey as far as she can with you, and it is as she desires."

King Ozias and Queen Oadira spent time with their children as they prepared to leave. The boys wanted to join them, but Oadira knew this was a journey for her and Ozias alone. Lyshyla would often join them, offering advice and words of wisdom.

"We can travel long distances through the Nibiru tunnels if we are going to get to Nereid's monument," Oadira said, looking at the map she had gotten long before from the archives.

"Why is Nereid's Monument so important to this realm? Why in particular is it important to Olokun and Yemoja?" Onika asked.

Lyshyla poured everyone some hot tea and sat beside Ozias. "Nereid is the wife of Nier. As a symbol of his love and devotion, he built her a monument and gave her the sodalite relic, Okavango's heart, showing that she would always have his heart for time and eternity. That's why magic is draining from the realm.

Ishtar and Obatala called Nier and Nereid back to Andalusia. As a result, Oadira, your parents, Nergal and Ninqi, became the Watchers of his realm, which gave them the titles of emperor and empress of Nier's realm and Nereid's monument, until they were summoned as one of the four sets of queens and kings to live in Sahael. The last Watchers of this realm were Oadira's grandparents, who were killed by Captain Lynch and his crew. When Empress Yemoja and Emperor Olokun leave Nier's realm, this kingdom will need new Watchers to look over it once again, which is why you and Ozias will become its protectors."

"Are there any new Watchers to take their place, other than us?" Oadira asked.

"No," Lyshyla said.

"What happens if we don't find any other stewards that can reign in our stead?" Oadira asked.

"Then, when we return to the city of Nieth and the Palace of Nieth, you and King Ozias will become the new Watchers and have to stay in the realm forever," Lyshyla answered. "Both of you have Watcher blood running through your veins. Both of you have the blood of ancients, and one of you is pure-blooded ancient."

"I didn't realize how important Nier's realm was to Aarde," Ozias said.

Oadira nodded, wondering how they could return to Sahael and fulfill all the prophecies regarding that dominion, while appeasing all the prophesies regarding Nier's Realm at the same time. "I learned that the magic from Nier's realm is what gives people eternal life," she said eventually. "Without that magic in Nier's realm, all the bloodlines will begin to have mortal lives and age every year like other Aardian.s If that were to happen, there would be no one left in the four realms to serve the people in Sahael, Alkebulan, and the generations that follow."

“Where does all of this magic come from?” Oshún asked, pulling his long dreadlocks into a twisted tail behind his ears.

“The magic that used to pump through Neolithic’s chamber and Nullify’s gate before spreading through Nier’s realm is what sustains the vitality of rivers, lakes, and oceans throughout all of Aarde,” Lyshyla said. “As Emperor Olokun has taught many times over the years, if the waters die, so will the surface because the waters sustain the surfaces and all life on Aarde. Without Nier’s realm, the other realms would cease to exist.”

Oadira thought to herself about all that had transpired over the past sixteen years, all the discussions with the divine rulers, all the smiles and laughter. Nier’s Realm was a beautiful place, worthy of survival.

“Without magic in this realm, there is no way the Nairohenge Gates can be activated?” she asked.

“I don’t understand their true purpose yet,” Lyshyla said. “But I feel they will be instrumental in helping restore Nier’s realm. All four of the realms must be in order and in proper balance, including the magic within Aarde and within the other three realms. The magic that comes from Nullify’s gate, through Nebuchadnezzar’s portal, and Nabopollassar’s sapphire seal is the same magic that allows the other three realms to operate efficiently. That magic is dwindling for every Watcher in the other three realms. Once magic is no longer produced and flowing in Nier’s realm, it will no longer sustain the other realms.”

“Which is why it is time for our journey to begin, my husband,” Oadira said, taking Ozias’ hand.

As soon as Onika’s 16th birthday celebration had ended a few days later, Oadira hugged her sons goodbye. They had long been taller than her, even Onika, but she still saw them as the little boys who would run into her and Ozias’ bedroom and jump on the bed to wake them up.

Oadira, and Ozias said their goodbyes to Oshún, Oxum, and Oya. Oadira told Oshún to watch over his little brother the entire time they were gone. Lyshyla also gave them hugs, and Oadira and Ozias said their goodbyes to Emperor Olokun and Empress Yemoja.

"Since the moment I arrived, this realm has been dying and decaying at a slow rate, affecting the environment all across Aarde," Oadira said to the rulers of Nier. "I will do all that is within my power to help restore the kingdom of my ancestors. I will find Okavango's heart."

"And we will welcome you back once you are successful," Emperor Olokun smiled. "You will always have a home here, for as long as Nier's Realm survives under the sun."

Oadira, Ozias, and Lyshyla left Nier's realm the same way they had entered over 16 years before, through the tunnel and seal, past the floating water barrier. Looking up through a transparent tunnel, they smelled fresh saltwater of the Nambissian Sea, seeing waves crash on the shore beyond the barrier. The vitality of the blue water seemed somehow diminished in Oadira's eyes, as if life itself were slowly being taken from the ocean.

They left the seashore and entered the stone tunnels of Nibiru, resting at clearings for a few hours and then continuing on for days at a time. The same colorful stones lit up the tunnel walls as they had 16 years before. Occasionally they came upon small groups of Treeps, who they slaughtered immediately each time to make sure not larger groups were ever alerted to their presence.

Eventually they reached the first metal door with its handprints and eternal flame burning, It was here that the Orishan bloodline had been awakened and the people of Iceoth had gained their abilities. Not far from here had been the battle with the giant spider Treeps that had killed and carried away dozens of people.

It all felt like a lifetime ago, and Oadira wondered if their people had ever made it to the barrio wall around Sahale. Had Ossa been successful inleading them home? Oadira hoped she would learn the answer soon enough.

They all rested and sat around Nile's cerulean flame to stay warm, talking about old times and what needed to be done.

"I still can't get over how depleted the ocean seemed," Ozias commented as he ate dried fruit from his backpack. "It was as if the very lifeforce of the water was being taken. I know Emperor Olokun has told us over the years that disasters continue around the world, but I could feel it when we looked at the sea. Is this magic tied to the events happening with open bodies of water? If these calamities are happening over Aarde, killing thousands of people, whose bodies are floating everywhere on the seas, the Ennead I'm sure are having difficulty keeping up due to so much death."

"These are the Signs of the Times that are upon us," Lyshyla suggested. "They will stop, but these events aren't happening by chance. It's why we must continue moving until an opportunity presents itself. Let's press on first thing in the morning."

At daybreak, Oadira, Ozias, and Lyshyla continued traveling through the last tunnel that emptied into an underwater bubble pocket at the bottom of a large lake. Fish and sea animals swam above them through the filtered light. Schools of fish, turtles, and all manner of large sharks, whales, and dolphins all seemed to be living in harmony with each other.

"This oasis of life is resilient. It's incredible," Lyshyla said, touching the water above her with her finger. "According to the maps given to us by the Empress, this lake should be where Nereid's Monument lies. Oadira and Ozias, please use your Orishan abilities to communicate with the fish. By seeing through their eyes we may more easily discover the monument's location."

Oadira blinked her eyes as the tattoos on her arms glowed blue. She suddenly felt cold water against scales, the unblinking eyes of a carp gazing through the clear water.

"I see Nereid's monument," Ozias said. "It's over the lake at the corner of the trenches. It's in ruins. A good portion of it is now underwater."

"Then let us get going," Lyshyla said.

They entered through the barrier, breathing the water as easily as air; bodies adapting to the cold environment. The lake was beautiful, the water clear and clean, showing its vibrant, fluorescent colors and all kinds of fish. They swam quickly, approaching from a distance. Just as Ozias had seen, whatever monument and underwater structures had once existed, now lie in complete ruin, like a beautiful jar that had been dropped onto hard stone.

This place—it's been completely destroyed! Ozias said telepathically.

What happened? Oadira asked.

The Narsans destroyed this sacred location and killed all the people in the monument, Lyshyla answered. *They broke the dams and flooded what remained, which is why most of it is now under the lake.*

Why would they do such a thing? Oadira asked as she gazed over the broken stones and flowing seaweed that now grew through the cracks.

This is where Nzingha's sapphire key used to be housed, Lyshyla said. *It seems that the Narsans left no stone unturned in their destruction of this monument on the orders of Lord Commander Natas. The Narsans want to destroy anything that doesn't enhance their culture and can minimize Black culture. They have no culture and seek to whitewash everything to fit in with their forced way of life. They killed everyone on Lord Commander Natas's orders.*

Why? Oadira asked.

Sometimes the best-kept secrets are the ones without witnesses. The dead can't speak because they sing the song of the dead. There's no reason for such barbaric actions! Nereid's monument provides Sahael with the ability to fuel Alkebulans with infinite resources. Nereid's monument also serves as one of the four pillars that help activate the Nairostone Gates, allowing hundreds at a time the ability to travel in large groups.

I can see what looks like an entrance over there, Ozias said, pointing toward what looked like an archway that had partially collapsed.

The three of them swam over the rubble toward the entryway. As they swam inside, they saw why the doorway had not fully collapsed. Behind it was a round stone seal ten feet across acting as the true doorway to the monument. A Marula Tree adorned the surface with an eight-pointed star above. In the center of the star was a picture of Sahael as a large, bright sapphire stone. The sapphires started to glow gradually.

There's a seal on the entrance shaped like Sahael's Marula Tree, Oadira pointed out.

It's the same seal in the Nibiru tunnels and all over Nier's realm, similar to the 'N' we saw in the caverns of Iceoth, Ozias said, scratching his beard.

This is Sahael's seal, Lyshyla said. She floated closer, running her fingers across the embossed surface. *It consists of a large Marula with an eight-point star representing the eight bloodlines of Sahael.*

There are two sets of handprints for entry, just like the other barriers. We need to place our hands on the images, Oadira said.

Ozias and Oadira placed their hands in the spaces. They both immediately started to feel a deep connection to Nier's realm. The entrance opened and Nereid's guardian appeared before them as a transparent, ghostly image of an ebony woman that stood eight-feet tall. She was gorgeous and well built, with ivory teeth, and long dreadlocks to the middle of her shoulders.

I am Nereid wife of Nier, keeper of the monument, the spirit messenger spoke to their minds. *Are you of the holy bloodline looking to complete the Trials of Ogum and become a Watcher?*

Oadira and Ozias nodded their heads.

We ask for the right to complete the trials, Oadira said. *We seek Okavango's heart.*

Only one pure-blooded ancient is allowed to enter my monument. Who will it be? Nereid asked.

We can go no further, Lyshyla said, touching Ozias' arm. *Ozias and I will have to stay here. Only you can attempt the Trials, Oadira. We must wait here until you return.*

How will I know what to do? Oadira asked.

Nereid motioned for Oadira to swim past her into the dark space beyond. *That is for you to find out on your own. Please enter. I won't repeat myself.*

Oadira made eye contact with Ozias and Lyshyla and then entered right away without hesitation. Nereid turned back into her cerulean Aardian form and dissipated into blue mist that entered into her monument.

Oadira swam into the darkness, eventually reaching a stone platform that exited the water. She breathed deeply of the stale air and looked around as she let the water drip from her body. The space was large, with only enough light to see directly around her.

Old stone tiles made up the floor; cracked and ancient.

The ghostly blue form of Nereid appeared in front of Oadira once more.

"The path before you has been revealed," Nereid said, voice echoing through the dark room. "At the end of this long pathway is a pedestal that will allow you the ability to accept all three of Ogum's Trials. They will challenge you and make you uncomfortable…completely vulnerable. Do you wish to continue?"

"Okay, I'll walk down to the pedestal at the end of the hall."

Nereid's ghostly form coalesced into a ball of light that moved in front of Oadira, lighting the path. Oadira made her way through the blackness, occasionally catching a glimpse of the walls around her. She appeared to be in a stone corridor. Only the sound of dripping water and her own footsteps reached her ears. An ornate pedestal carved from marble appeared from the darkness. A silver ring with a purple stone of iolite sat on the pedestal, similar to the rings Oadira wore on her fingers.

What do I do next? Do I take this ring? Oadira thought.

The light glowed in front of her, offering no instructions.

"I'll just take it for safekeeping," Oadira said to the light, hoping for some small token of Nereid's understanding. Only silence answered her statement. She placed the ring inside the pouch on her hip,

The pedestal retracted into the ground revealing a series of stones behind it forming an arrow that pointed to he left.

Oadira followed the arrow and discovered a doorway against a wall that stretched up into the darkness. In an instant, she started to feel connected to the rivers, lakes, and oceans of Aarde. The solid structure of the wall became a transparent lapis lazuli color, allowing her to enter Nereid's monument. Upon entering,

Oadira saw a vast and large open area several miles wide, like a stone dome overhead. Water covered the floor four inches deep, smelling of dead fish and other sea animal carcasses floating on the water. Debris was everywhere, and the structure seemed unstable, ready to collapse at any moment. Oadira looked out over the horizon, feeling overwhelmed. She started walking and continued walking for another hour until she came upon a broken section of floor that had been completely flooded. She swam across, pushing aside some swollen beast corpse, and from there continued walking.

It looked like the space could go on for days, weeks, or months. How could an interior space be so limitless? All the while the ball of light floated around her, lighting the area within its glow, sometimes brighter, sometimes dim. Time seemed to have no meaning here as Oadira walked and swam, climbed and leaped, for what felt like days in the dark.

She came upon another section of stone flooring, broken and pitched to the left and right as if shifted by an earthquake. Water geysers shot up from the ground in bursts of superhot steam. Oadira leaped out of their way, but every step forward seemed to ignite another boiling eruption. The temperatures of the geysers increased, heating the air inside Nereid's monument until it was stifling.

"You need to get out of this area as soon as you can or risk being trapped by the cursed fountains," Nereid's voice spoke from the light. "You need to be careful and figure out a way to maneuver through these geysers."

"What happens if I'm caught in one of them?" Oadira asked.

"Then the geysers will burn off all of your skin, leaving only your bones behind," Nereid said.

At least it would only be a physical punishment, Oadira

thought. *Some fates are worse than pain and suffering, especially in a place like this.*

Oadira did all she could to navigate through the geyser plains. The surrounding water grew increasingly deeper and deeper, until she started swimming once more. Ripples suddenly pushed against her from the opposite direction.

Something was coming in her direction.

The water swirled around her, spinning Oadira uncontrollably until she felt dizzy, lost, and disoriented. It wasn't a creature moving in the water, it was the water itself moving like an angry beast. She hovered on the edge of consciousness for a moment until the water once again settled itself.

Before she could reorient herself, the water pulled her under. Using her Orishan artes, the darkness receded and Oadira could see razor-sharp, pointed rocks protruding out of the sea floor, easily sharp enough to pierce through her skin. The current spun her toward the rocks. With great effort, Oadira swam against the tide, arms and feet pumping as fast as she could move them. Even her hydrokenisis could barely nudge her forward out of the whirlpool's embrace. Just as her foot touched against one of the jagged rocks, Oadira escaped the current and swam back to the surface.

Pulling herself out of the water onto a series of broken stone pillars, Oadira gasped and heaved, muscles burning, lungs screaming.

"You can't rest," the light spoke. "The walls from behind you are closing in. You have to keep moving forward. There is no going back or stopping; only moving forward."

"Understood," Oadira acknowledged. She wearily stood and looked around. The light from Nereid's presence reflected off an object not too far ahead; what appeared to be a large spectrolitecolored obelisk that stretched upward into the darkness. How tall was it? Oadira had no way of even guessing. She couldn't even see the ceiling anymore, and when she had, it was so distant the individual stones couldn't even be seen.

"Nassir's Obelisk," Oadira whispered.

"You should hurry, daughter of Sahael," Nereid spoke from the disembodied light.

The sound of stone scraping against stone caught Oadira's attention. She looked back, seeing the walls moving toward her. She had thought Nereid's comment about the walls closing in was metaphorical, but obviously there was nothing metaphorical about this strange monument.

Oadira started running toward the obelisk, feet splashing through puddles as she charged forward. As she drew closer, the sound of swirling water met her ears. Just in time she saw Nassir's obelisk surrounded by a whirlpool far too large to jump across. The mass of water swirled and churned, threatening to sweep away anyone who entered. If this whirlpool was anything like what Oadira had faced in the water a few minutes before, she stood no chance of survival.

Oadira looked around, trying to come up with any ideas of how she could make it on the platform below the obelisk.

I can use my Orishan artes to conjure up a hook shot to pull myself up to the structure, Oadira said to herself. *With an energetic rope and hook, I should be able to pull myself across.*

It was worth a shot as the walls continued drawing closer with the threat of pushing her into the whirlpool.

Oadira ran and jumped off the solid ground, shooting her hook shot into the sides of the obelisk. She used the conjured hook and rope to swing her toward the large structure in the center of the whirlpool. Oadira pulled with all her strength, swinging across the whirlpool, feeling the water spray on her feet as she drew near enough to be pulled in. With one last pull of her strong arms, Oadira bypassed the whirlpool and slammed into the obelisk with full force. The air from her lungs was pushed from her body as she slumped to the stone ground, mere feet from the roiling water.

"What now?" she breathed.

The light twisted and formed into the translucent form of Nereid. The luminous woman simply pointed up with her index finger and reformed into the cold light.

Oadira looked up at the obelisk. She couldn't see the top, but it seemed to go on forever, just like the room itself.

"I guess we climb," she mumbled.

Using her artes, Oadira morphed the single rope into a rope ladder that enabled her to climb up the obelisk. Every dozen feet or so she would extend her energies and reform the ladder. After an hour, she could no longer see the top of the structure, nor the bottom. She climbed in a nothing-space of air and darkness, the small silent light her only companion.

Then from out of nowhere, Spear-like projectiles started firing out of the large structure, coming at Oadira with punishing speed.

Another test of her skill and ingenuity.

Oadira pivoted, almost losing her grip on the rope, before using their artes to deflect most of spikes.

Now more wary than ever, Oadira continued climbing, hours bleeding into each other as sweat stung her eyes. Her muscles ached.

Just as she thought she couldn't climb another rung of the ladder, Oadira reached the top and slumped herself onto the flat space with a grunt.

She lay there, in and out of consciousness, no longer aware of how long it had been since she'd seen Ozias and Lyshyla; her children were nothing more than a dream, and Sahael was a myth; Natas a demon from a nightmare. How long had it been since she'd eaten? Was food even real, or was it something she had imagined? Was she even real, or simply someone else's dream given flesh for a moment before they woke back up?

Her eyes opened and she took a deep breath. Oadira sat up and looked down on the blackness below her. The silence was punishing. Before her on the platform stood an obsidian pillar, tall and shiny.

"This is the obelisk?" she asked the light. "I thought this tower was the obelisk. What do I do now? Where is Okavango's heart?"

The light simply floated before her.

Oadira approached Nassir's obelisk. As she touched the smooth surface, three circles lit up; two small circles attached to a larger circle in the middle. The circles were open holes reaching back into the obelisk like infinite openings.

"What do these three circles mean?" Oadira asked, knowing the light of Nereid's spirit would be no help. She had to figure it out on her own.

Oadira noticed Nebiriau's bracelet and Njiru's ring on her finger had lit up like the circles. A light seemed to emanate from the pouch on her hip as well. She opened it up and found the ring she had taken from the pillar glowing along with the circles too.

"What does this all mean? I don't know what to do," Oadira said.

Oadira thought as hard as she could, trying to figure out what to do. She looked at the circles again and again until a thought came to her. She placed the ring she had found on the pedestal inside the smallest hole. Then she removed her own ring and placed it in the next largest circular hole. Finally, she took off her bracelet and deposited it inside the biggest opening.

The platform shook all around her. She felt it descending into the blackness. Soon she heard the whirlpool churning below her until the platform stopped in the center of the whirlpool, water splashing up over the sides.

Then a single Nairo gate appeared from out of nowhere as a sphere of pure blue energy. A set of grandidierite eyes appeared at the top of the single Nairo gate.

The small light once again transformed into Nereid's spiritual essence. "Well done, daughter of Sahael."

"What do I do now?" Oadira asked. Suddenly her tattoos began to glow blue. "What does this mean?"

"Use what activated the Signs of the Times," Nereid answered.

"My eyes!" Oadira said.

Understanding what she needed to do, Oadira blinked her eyes twice, activating the Nairo gate. A set of stairs rose up from the platform and led to the entrance of the gate.

"Take your items and go in peace, daughter of Sahael," Nereid said. "You have proven yourself worthy and passed the trials, showing determination, stamina, and intelligence."

Oadira took Njiru's ring, Nebiriau's bracelet, and the pedestal ring from Nassir's obelisk before walking up the stairs. She looked back at Nereid's spirit, but saw nothing there, not even the light that had guided her.

"Nothing left to do now but step though, I guess," Oadira whispered. She could barely stand and wanted nothing more than to eat something and sleep for a week, but the last trial stood before her.

She still needed to find Okavango's heart. And it obviously wasn't here in the monument.

She nodded her head and walked through the portal.

CHAPTER VI

NEREID'S PALACE

Nier's realm, Nereid's inner sanctuary

Oadira appeared in a place where the walls were golden ivory and clean. A castle stood before her in the distance, sun shining above it, surrounded by green fields. Giraffes, lions, gazelles, and hyenas roamed the lands in large numbers.

"Where am I?" Oadira asked, strength slowly giving out as she swayed in the warm breeze.

"You're in No," a deep voice said to her right. Startled, Oadira jumped and looked over at a ten-foot-tall, four-hundred-pound man with a white afro, beard, and agate eyes standing in front of an iron gate. His rotund form implied a jolliness that Oadira didn't know whether to trust or not.

"Who are you?" Oadira asked.

"You are the guest here," the man smiled with a sense of regal entitlement about him. "Who are you?"

"My name is Oadira Ocnus, Queen of Iceoth, Daughter of Nergal, High Queen of Sahael," Oadira replied.

"Congratulations on making it through the Watcher Trials,"

the giant man said as he rubbed his hands together, licking his lips. "I am Ogum, one of the Wiru. Why have you come?"

"I've come because Nier's realm is dying," Oadira answered.

"How is that possible?" Ogum asked, eyes widening. "The previous caretakers, Emperor Oso and Empress Osa, the steward and stewardess of Nier's realms, were watching over the dominion until their granddaughters were old enough to run the kingdom."

"The previous caretakers, my grandfather and grandmother, were killed to save the Negralli people," Oadira said.

"How did they die, child?" Ogum asked with real worry on his face.

"They died saving the Negralli people by giving up Nzingha's sapphire key," Oadira said.

"What would cause them to do such a thing?" Ogum asked in obvious shock.

"Captain Lynch invaded Nier's realm and made his way past the Negralli gates and its defenses with First Commander Shu of the Ennead Legion," Oadira said with tears falling down her cheeks. She fell to her knees as her exhaustion finally got the better of her. She slumped there in the grass, body a tired mass of twisted muscle and sinew.

"What did Captain Lynch do?" Ogum asked. "I can tell you are tired, but I must know."

"He forced their hands by threatening to kill every Negralli in Nier's realm," Oadira answered, closing her eyes. "Captain Lynch asked for Nzingha's sapphire key for reasons we know not. The stewards wanted to prevent the slaughter of the people. They gave up Nzingha's sapphire key to save the lives of the Negralli people, but they were killed regardless."

Ogum slammed his fist on his iron gates, again making Oadira jump in surprise. She looked up at him, seeing throbbing veins along his neck.

"What happened next?" Ogum asked, leaning over toward Oadira's hunched, kneeling form.

"The sea gods Yemoja and Olokun gave up their godhood to take over as the new stewards of the realm. They sacrificed themselves so that the people could live to help rebuild Nier's realm," Oadira answered.

"So, is this the main reason you have come, to find a means of replacing them by taking part in the Watcher Trials?" Ogum asked.

"Yeah," Oadira answered nervously.

"There has to be more to it than that," Ogum said as his eyes narrowed, and he blew out his cheeks.

"What do you mean?" Oadira asked.

"To keep Nier's realm running, they're using their lifeforce to help sustain life, which means it has taken a toll on their bodies through wear and tear. Magic is the lifeforce of the realm. They will eventually die along with all life in the oceans," Ogum said. He let out a *humph*. "What is it you seek?"

"I seek the ancient sodalite relic," Oadira said. "Okavango's Heart."

"You seek the heart of the north that can help you restore Nier's realm. The Signs of the Times are truly upon us," Ogum said. "Follow me."

Oadira stood shakily and followed Ogun through the iron gates into a courtyard full of rose bushes and other flowers. Ogun sat down on one of his benches and motioned for Oadira to do the same.

"The heart is powerful," Ogun said as Oadira sat across from him on a stone bench.

"I don't know if it can restore Nier's realm, but it's needed to help save Aarde," Oadira said.

"I understand," Ogum said. He clapped his hands and a guard dressed in golden armor and a red cape walked out from behind a large rose bush. He bowed to Ogum. "Bring it to me," the giant white-haired man said in his deep voice.

The guard ran off and returned quickly carrying a large wooden chest to Ogum.

"I have what it is you seek, Okavango's Heart," Ogum said as he pulled a large blue gemstone on a golden chain from the chest and placed it around his neck. Okavango's Heart shone with magnificence, beauty, and immeasurable power. Cuts ran along its surface, splitting the large stone into at least four pieces Oadira could see. "The heart was placed in my care by Nereid herself right before she and Nier ascended to Andalusia. The pieces of the heart are drawn together, held united like magnets." He looked down at the jewel and touched it with his index finger. "Narim called it the heart of the sea, after ripping his own heart from his chest and handing it to Nier as a wedding gift to give to Nereid, renaming it Okavango out of respect. Okavango's Heart will help restore magic back to Nier's realm, and beyond. What do you know of the Heart?"

"Only what I've read in Nygaard's prophecy. There are eight pieces, all meant to serve the people of Alkebulan and the enslaved people of Aarde. A queen of Sahael must use it in the service of others."

Ogum nodded his large head, smiling as if he knew something Oadira didn't.

"I love prophesies," he said. "They are always pointed

enough to show a direction, but vague enough for people to get the details wrong."

"What details do I have wrong?" Oadira asked.

"You'll learn, Queen Oadira, that even the wise have not been told everything. The gods lay out a path, but it is up to each of us to choose to walk it. You think the gods wanted Natas to do what he did? Of course not, but he chose to do it, and they knew he would make that choice. In knowing, they set things in motion that would allow us to rectify things, if we chose to do so. You may think you're the first person to set out on this quest. You're not. You're simply the first to choose to come this far and not give up. That makes you special in my eyes. You may have the Heart if you ask for it. Though it won't come without sacrifice."

"What are you asking in return for Okavango's Heart?" Oadira asked. She was too tired to attempt any sort of challenge, but at least she could find out what it would take.

"Okavango's heart requires a heavy price," Ogum said as he made eye contact with Oadira.

"What price is that?" Oadira asked.

"It requires you to take over Nier's realm, relinquishing Olokun and Yemoja to help restore life to Sahaedron. Do you understand what I'm asking?" Ogum asked.

"Do I have a choice? Does my husband the king have a choice?" Oadira asked.

"There's always a choice," Ogum said.

"I'll do whatever it takes to save Nier's realm when the time comes," Oadira said. "It has been my home for almost 17 years. But I have other duties as well; other prophecies to fulfill. Other places I want to go. How do I act when one action contradicts another? When one choice eliminates so many other choices?"

Ogum smiled and chuckled lightly. "Such is life, Queen Oadira Ocnus of Iceoth, Daughter of Nergal, High Queen of Sahael, and Empress of Nier's Realm. The question remains. Will you save those you can save now, or let them suffer to save others in the future?"

It was a pointed question to be sure. The future was always unknown. Prophecies would always contradict. Would she choose to help the people she knew she could help at this moment, or sacrifice them for others somewhere down the road, who Oadira might not be able to save anyway?

"I will choose to save Nier's Realm," Oadira nodded. As she spoke, her body seemed to relax, and all tension melted away. It was the right decision.

"Do you understand what you're doing?" Ogun asked. "What about your husband? Does he have a choice? Are you clear what is needed in return?"

"I understand, even if it means I have to give up going to Sahael," Oadira said sadly. Ever since she met Solomon and learned her destiny, all she ever wanted to do was to get to Sahael. It was within reach and now she had to put her plans on hold, possibly forever, to save another people.

"You would make the decision then, even for those you love who would not wish to remain in Neir's Realm with you?"

Oadira sunk back into the bench, eyes blinking slowly. "They may think what I've done is unacceptable and can't happen. They may demand that we be allowed to leave Nier's realm together."

"That simply just can't happen, at least for you and your husband, if you take this heart back to Nieth," Ogum said.

"But then, what of Sahael?" Oadira asked, head shaking. "If I stay in Nier's realm, then the Negralli will die, as will the three other realms. The gods themselves have spoken it."

"And their words are rarely incorrect."

"Then why," Oadira countered with more strength, "am I being forced to choose between one realm and another? Between the lives of one people and another?"

Ogun grinned and rubbed his thumb against the gem around his neck. "Such choices are why you are here and others are not; why you made it through the unending snares and mental fatigue of Nereid's Monument when others give up. It is not your blood, as others might say. It is you, the woman you are and the choices you make. It is not our bloodline that makes us champions, queens, and servants to our people. It is who we are and our choices. What do you choose?"

"I will do what I have to do and remain in Nier's realm." Oadira said.

"Then I am certain you will figure something out regarding how to save everyone else," Ogum said. "The gods have their eyes on you for a reason, and I think it will be because you will be able to solve problems that would crush lesser minds." Ogum rubbed his white beard for a moment. "How can I help?"

"I'm…not sure what to even ask for," Oadira answered.

Ogum nodded. "My home is safe and intact, but my sister's monument is in ruins, and as the magic dies, my brother-in-law's realm will follow. I made a promise to them years ago after Nereid gave me Okavango's heart as she ascended that I would always be there for the people to earn my right for ascension when the time was right."

"You're Nereid's brother," Oadira nodded. She now understood why he had been entrusted with such a sacred and powerful item.

"I am."

"So, you are of the royal line?" Oadira asked.

"I am."

Oadira breathed slowly. All weariness faded from her mind. "You have a blood right to be a steward of Nier's realm the same as I do."

Another smile filled the large man's face. "I do."

"And if I were to ask you," Oadira said slowly, "would you take mine and my husband's place so we can save the other three realms?"

"You would ask for help?" Ogum asked.

"Yes! Of course, yes! It would allow us to enter Sahael and perform the works that will end all of this suffering."

Ogun leaned toward Oadira as a butterfly flitted in front of his face. "You are powerful, Queen Oadira Ocnus of Iceoth, Daughter of Nergal, High Queen of Sahael, and Empress of Nier's Realm. I have found during my very long existence that few people who are considered powerful will ask for help, seeing it as a weakness. So, I ask again, are you seeking my aid?"

"Yes," Oadira repeated without hesitation. "Asking for help is not a weakness. Perhaps if my people had asked the other bloodlines for help in generations past, they wouldn't have been so divided, and Lord Commander Natas never would have succeeded in destroying them."

"Such is wisdom," Ogum nodded. "I can steward Nier's realm, allowing you and your family the ability to return to Sahael."

Oadira smiled. "Why would you do this for us?"

"I would do it for all people because I was asked to help by a powerful queen. My energy is full. I can use my lifeforce to help sustain Nier's realm until you can find a way to save everyone you wish to save," Ogum said.

"Thank you, Ogum. Thank you."

"No," Ogum said, head swiveling back and forth. "It is you who should be thanked. You see yourself as a servant, not a ruler. You ask for help, not caring what others will think of you. Pride does not dictate your actions, rather compassion. You are worthy of your crown, and that of Sahael, should the time come. You have passed my test, and I will see you are given the opportunity to save the peoples of Aarde."

"What are the next steps?" Oadira asked.

"We head back to Nier's realm and Nieth Palace," Ogum said.

"How?"

"I have the means to travel there, worry not," Ogum said. He clapped his hands again and the guard returned. Ogum handed him the chest. "Tell them it is time," he whispered to the guard. "The trials have been passed and a worthy queen is tired and wants to return home."

After Ogum finished speaking, the guard ran off toward the palace in the distance. A few minutes later, several people emerged from the front gates and began walking toward Oadira and Ogum.

"That is Nereid's Palace," Ogum said, waving his hand toward the mansion. "Do you see the beautiful creature approaching us now? She is of the Ouadane tribe, and is my wife Ora, whose original name was Sarah Baartman."

As the people drew closer, Oadira saw a large woman who stood eight feet tall with long, white, braided hair in cornrows with elaborate designs, accompanied by a Medjay Gate Guardian who stood nearly nine feet tall and was slender with long dreadlocks and ivory-colored teeth. A few other women followed Ora, dressed in robes, equally as tall and beautiful as their matron.

Oadira stood, wondering what the custom in Nereid's Palace was regarding guests.

Ogum got up and walked toward his wife Ora. They embraced and then spoke for a few minutes, after which the other women gathered around Ora, looking down at her head and the designs braided into her hair.

"My wife is a Navigator," Ogum said to Oadira. "As it was done of old, the patterns for travel are transcribed in her braids of how to navigate us safely back to Nieth."

"What about my husband Ozias and Educator Lyshyla?" Oadira asked. "I left them underwater at the monument entrance."

"Please hand me the pedestal ring you took from Nereid's monument," Ogum said.

Oadira pulled it from her belt pouch and handed it to him.

Ogum rubbed Njiru's iolite ring, opening Nebuchadnezzar's sapphire portal.

"What's going on?" Oadira asked.

"I am using Njiru's power through the iolite ring to bring Educator Lyshyla and your husband here, so that we can travel directly to Nier's realm," Ogum answered. "Soon, you will learn how to use this power as well. Your ring is of the same energy as this. It requires will power, knowledge of space and time, and the years of life that allow mastery over such things.

"Why not just use the ring to take us Neir's Realm directly?" Oadira asked. "Why use the Nairohenge gates at all?"

"Njiru's iolite ring grants its wearers—you, your husband, and I—the ability to transport only purebloods. We'd have to leave Lyshyla behind; she may share some cursed blood and must travel through the Nairohenge Gates back to Nier's realm." Ogum closed his eyes. "You say you left your husband and the Educator underwater at the entrance to the monument, but that would be months ago now. Let me search for their auras for a moment."

"Months ago?" Oadira questioned. "What are you talking about? It's been maybe a day since I left them."

"Your trials were mental as well as physical," Ogum said, eyes still closed. "The pressure on your mind was great indeed, stretching time in all directions. You endured much without realizing it. Months will have passed since you entered the trials."

Months? Where would Ozias and Lyshyla be after months? Did they think she was dead? Had they returned brokenhearted to Nier's Realm to inform the boys of their mother's death?

"Ah, here they are," Ogum said with a smile.

The shiny blue portal became translucent and Oadira saw Ozias and Lyshyla sitting next to a fire on the shores of a lake eating fish and mussels.

"Ozias!" Oadira shouted. Her husband's head shot up, followed by a large smile. He and Lyshyla rushed forward and through the portal, embracing Oadira with shouts of joy and reunion.

"What happened?" Ozias asked. "You're okay! I'm so happy to see you, my love!"

"I have lots of questions," Lyshyla said.

"You did it! You completed the Watcher Trials," Ozias said, hugging Oadira again.

"How long have you been waiting?" Oadira asked. "Ogum here said it's been months? I wasn't even aware."

Ozias nodded. "After you entered the tunnel, the door closed behind you and the spirit of Nereid appeared to us saying it would be several months before you emerged from the trials. We built a shelter on the shores of the lake and have been hunting and fishing ever since, waiting for you to return. I knew you could do it!"

"Good job, Oadira," Lyshyla beamed. "You've truly earned your place as the high queen of Sahael."

"We don't have much time. The Signs of the Times are upon us, and Nier's realm needs rebuilding," Ogum said. "I will accompany you all back to Nieth, as the queen and I have agreed. My wife will join me."

Ora led the group to a nearby grove where large blocks of well-hewn stone stood like doorways in a circle. Ora stood in the center, chanting in an unknown language, Her guard and the other women repeated her words until the air became electrified. Skin tingling, Oadira knew that these gates would soon activate, allowing them to return to her children.

As the chanting reached a crescendo, A magnificent circular portal opened, twenty feet wide, swirling in blue, purple, and yellow light.

"Let us go," Ogum nodded toward the gateway. "Neir's Realm awaits."

He stepped forward and Oadira followed, hand-in-hand with Ozias. Together they walked through the Nairohenge Gates, arriving back in Nieth.

After a flash of light and a feeling of weightlessness, Oadira stepped into the central plaza of Neith city. One of the four central gates had activated, coming up out of the ground and acting as a mirror of the stones that had just encircled them. The people rejoiced and celebrated their return. The Nubian guard surrounded the newly arrived group immediately, assuming protection over the king and queen once more along with Ogum and Ora.

Every Negralli in Nieth bowed as a sign of respect when Ogum took his first steps.

"You all may rise," Ogum said, who took Okavango's heart from around his neck and placed it in the hands of Oadira. "Okavango's heart holds the power to restore life to this realm, and all of life within the seas, rivers, lakes, ponds, and streams. The heart of the sea is made up of nine pieces; you will need all nine pieces if you want to fully restore Aarde and get to Sahael. When the time is right, you'll know how to use them. As the new stewards of Nier's realm, we are handing Okavango's sapphire heart over to the both of you. It's up to you both what you choose to do with the nine pieces. It's yours now," Ogum said, bowing to Oadira.

Ogum handed Okavango's sapphire heart to Oadira, and her eyes and tattoos all started to glow. The power that emanated from her was on clear display for all who watched. They immediately fell to both knees, showing complete and total submission to the new rulers.

"After I place these stones," Oadira began, "We will leave this people in the stewardship or Ogum and Ora, so we may once again liberate all of Aarde and open the gates of Sahael once more!"

The people roared their approval, cheering and shouting that Sahael would rise again.

Oadira held Okavango's sapphire heart in her hands and could hear the waters running in between the Nairohenge Gates and on the sides of the streets. She walked over to the streaming waters and removed one of the nine pieces, placing it in the stream. Immediate magic and energy passed through the waters.

"The Nairohenge Gates are rising from the ground," Ozias said.

"Four of the nineteen gates that make up Nairohenge are now active," Lyshyla said.

Ogum raised his hands to the sky. "The currents will carry the magical power in the waters everywhere that water touches. In turn, it will rejuvenate the lands and help restore life to the dying oceans in Aarde. It's a slow and gradual process, ensuring that the Signs of the Times provide you with the time you need to avoid being tracked and followed by those who are hunting you."

Oadira and Ozias were then greeted by their children Oshún, Oxum, Oya, and Onika, who ran as quickly as he could toward their mother and father. Empress Yemoja and Emperor Olokun followed behind the children as they rejoiced to see each other and were all reunited as a family.

"Welcome back. I see that you've safely completed the Watcher Trials," Empress Yemoja said, relief on her face.

"Yes, we have returned with the means to save the realm and the people," Oadira said.

"During your time away, a ship was refurbished for you to travel to Timbuktu if necessary." Emperor Olokun said. "The Negralli people helped fix it up by compiling all the destroyed ships into one. You can use it to pass through the Nairohenge Gates and continue your journey from there."

"But for now, we will celebrate and enjoy a moment of peace," Empress Yemoja replied. "Let us eat and rest, reestablish bonds between parents and children, and bask in the bright sunlight of our blessed realm."

After a feast, and several days of preparation and time with family, Ogum asked to speak with Oadira and Lyshyla in Yemoja and Olokun's private quarters.

"Thank you all for coming," Ogum said as he stepped from the balcony overlooking the city. Olokun and Yemoja sat on a couch beside the window.

"The Nairohenge Gates are not activated on the other side

in Timbuktu and will not receive you," Olgum continued. "I have been trying to establish a connection, but there has been no response. My Njiru ring can't access Timbuktu, so we are facing a problem. I had hoped the gates in Timbuktu would still be manned and operational, but that is now obviously not the case. The Gates must be activated in each of the four realms and finally Sahael before they can be used for travel among the four realms. The Nairohenge Gates allow Sahael to protect all of Aarde and its people. When the Narsans invaded Sahael and destroyed Khartoum Palace, they killed many of the Builders, Navigators, and Medjay Gate Guardians, forcing the rest to go into hiding. This cut them off from their homeland of Sahael, so they chose exile rather than slaughter by the Narsans."

"There must be a way to save or find them," Oadira said to the group.

Lyshyla sat in one of the chairs. "What are the chances of finding one now? It's been almost 50 years since the fall of Sahael."

"During the assault on the lands of Alkebulan," Ogum replied, "the Navigators, Guardians, and the Nibiru escaped all over Aarde to avoid being followed. They traveled to unknown places, deactivating the Nairohenge Gates from behind them. The Nibiru must be found; without them, Sahael can't be restored, nor will it regain its ability to travel anywhere to keep Aarde safe."

Empress Yemoja stood from her seat on the couch. "You need to prepare as if they aren't going to be found. Chances are the Narsans hunted them all down and killed them,"

"In order to bring back gate travel, the twelve bloodlines must return to Sahael," Emperor Olokun said.

"I understand," Oadira said. "A gathering must take place. But how was it going to happen without the gates? We are supposed to enter Sahael and then open the wall barriers for the people."

"You will be guided to a solution, I'm sure," Ogum said with a smile. "You are good at solving problems. Remember, the first gathering was to be initiated by the four bloodlines created when the eight lineages were merged, which is why the Gathering must take place. The ancient Kemites wanted to protect all Alkebulans, Egyptians, and Sahaelians in Aarde. The ancient Kemites were stretched too thin, so the divines sent down the twelve tribes, who were scattered all over Alkebulan and Aarde. The Watchers were sent to guard the chosen, those who chose to serve the Alkebulan tribes that were sent down to Aarde. Ishtar and Obatala's fallen son Natas wanted to enslave and cleanse the Andalusians of Kemite blood, leading to him being cast out of Andalusia and sent to the outer realm of Nothing."

"I didn't know Natas wanted to cleanse his bloodline of Kemite blood," Oadira said.

"Lord Commander Natas wants to save his people and is willing to do whatever it takes," Lyshyla said.

Ogum leaned over and smelled a flower in a pot on the balcony. "Lord Commander Natas was able to escape by obtaining Njiru's onyx ring and then gaining control over the Ennead and persuading their minds that they would be better off on their own. So, they were separated from the Ancient Order to work as his personal army in western Aarde, severing themselves off from Eastern Aarde entirely by choice."

"We need to find out more about what's happened. The best way to do that is to get to Amit and restore Nier's connection to our history," Lyshyla said.

"Agreed," Oadira said. "But without the gates, there's nothing we can do."

Empress Yemoja held her index finger up. "There is one

way. When you returned from your quest to retrieve Okavango's Heart, I told you we had refurbished a ship to use to travel through the gates, but there was a secondary reason as well."

"Yes," Emperor Olokun nodded. "We feared the gates to Timbuktu might not function in the way we hoped. That being the case, the ship has been made ready to travel to Timbuktu by way of ocean current instead of the gates."

Lyshyla shook her head and stood back up. "One cannot simply sail to Timbuktu. The waters shift and swirl away from the hidden land. Plus, if you find the city at all, there are barriers, mists, and magics that entangle the mind. If we set off by ship, we will return here with nothing at best, and be lost for eternity in the depths at worst."

"We can guide you as best we can," Yemoja replied. "We will use our abilities to shift the currents, so you travel paths few others have sailed. It is our only option if we wish to free Sahael and all the peoples of Aarde."

Oadira paced for a moment. It seemed fate never made her path easy. And yet, over her adult life she had seen miracles in many circumstances. Her escape from Madame Lalaurie? A miracle. Her victory over the invaders of Iceoth? A miracle. A peaceful life with her husband and children in Neir's Realm? A miracle.

She was willing to put her faith in miracles one more time.

"We're going," Oadira said with a smile. "Me, Ozias, my children…and you, Lyshyla. We will sail to Timbuktu, solve whatever mysteries present themselves, and reunite our people in the lands of our inheritance. I have faith, and that faith will see me through."

No other words needed to be said. Ogum picked the flower he had been smelling and tossed it to Oadira with a deep laugh that jiggled his round belly and enormous frame.

“You are a queen of Sahael!” he bellowed. “I doubt any barrier will keep you from righting a world that has been injured.”

The next morning, they made their way to the docks where the ship was located. It was well crafted with fine wood and crisp white sails, but not large like the ships Oadira had sailed on previously. It would be comfortable, but not opulent. Yemoja, Olokun, and Ogum all helped load supplies to make sure Oadira and her family had all that they would need for their long, shadowy journey.

“Ora the Ouadane Navigator and Yasuké the Medjay Gate Guardian will accompany you to Timbuktu,” Ogum ordered. “Please, watch over my wife Ora as I send her with you. She is my rose pedal and the light of my long existence. Keep her safe on this unknown journey.”

“We will,” Ozias said.

“Thank you.” Lyshyla said. “If all goes well, they will at least be able to open the gates on the Timbuktu side.”

“They will,” Oadira said as she walked pasted them up the gangplank to the ship, followed by her four sons. “Have faith!”

“Have faith, Lyshyla,” young Onika grinned as he nudged Lyshyla’s shoulder.

Olokun and Yemoja returned to the sea, allowing magic and life to return to Nier’s realm for a short time. Ogum and his wife were now the stewards of the realm. The ten-foot-tall man waved as the former regents disappeared below the waves, and the ship to Timbuktu sailed into the morning sun.

“Good journey to you!” Ogum shouted.

Oadira waved back as the shore slowly receded on the horizon. The ship rocked back and forth as it departed to the great library and city of Timbuktu.

CHAPTER VII

TIMBUKTU

Nambissian Sea, Timbuktu

Over the next few days, the currents moved in a southwest direction despite the wind blowing almost constantly to the east. Yemoja and Olokun's assistance became more and more apparent to further they sailed. While traveling, the royal family took the time to catch up with each other as Ogum's crew controlled the ship, ensuring they made it safely to Timbuktu.

"The Nambissian Sea is full of history," Lyshyla said, observing the color return to the ocean. "The heart of the sea is filling it once more with life, beauty, and vibrance. Look at all the sea creatures returning from the deep—dolphins, whales, sharks, sea turtles, and more. They are now being protected once again by Olokun and Yemoja."

Oadira could feel the presence of Olokun and Yemoja helping them. The air itself tasted sweet and clean, often reminding her of Ymoja's perfume. Okavango's heart hung on its necklace around Oadira's neck at all times, like a trophy that would allow entrance to Timbuktu. She honestly had no idea what they would face, but the heart would stay with her and hopefully help in their journey. The royal family settled in as Oadira and Ozias made up for lost time with their children, learning about what they'd done during their months away.

"Onika was able to learn about his powers. Empress Yemoja tested him the same way you tested us," Oshún said as he sat in Oadira and Ozia's personal quarters eating some dried fruit.

"How did Onika do?" Oadira asked.

"He passed, making it look easier compared to when Oxum, Oya, and I had to fight you all those years ago. Emperor Olokun had to intervene to stop Onika. Onika is powerful and doesn't even realize it yet."

"That's good to know. We'll keep an eye on him closely," Ozias smiled, taking a bite of the fruit as well.

"While you were gone," Oshún explained. "I hoped I'd have time to hunt in the forests with my team, but you know how Olokun is. He and Lyshyla are both so interested in history and family lineage. One day I was preparing for a hunt when he told me my brothers were waiting for me back in the archives and I was to attend school until you and father returned. And so, for the last two months we attended school, helped rebuild the city after another earthquake, and learned all there was to know about Nier's realm. Emperor Olokun and Empress Yemoja kept us on a rigorous schedule. That was not fun but kept us extremely busy."

"That was good of Empress Yemoja to do. Please help your brothers on the top deck," Oadira said.

"Yes, Mother," Oshún said as he left their personal quarters.

Lyshyla entered just as Oshún stepped out. She bowed and then sat down where Oadira's son had been sitting moments before.

"Now that we're well beyond the borders of Nier's Realm,"

Lyshyla began, "I have questions about the Watcher Trials."

"I'm forbidden to speak about the Trials and can only speak to Ozias about them, per realm law," Oadira said candidly.

"I understand. What happened with Njiru's iolite ring?" Lyshyla asked.

"According to Ogum, it gives the emperor and empress the ability to open up Nebuchadnezzar's iolite portal anywhere in Aarde once the Nairohenge Gates in all four realms and Sahael are restored," Oadira said.

Lyshyla nodded and threw a piece of dried walnut in her mouth. "I understand with Nier's realm back in balance, it's only a matter of time before the typhoons, tsunamis, and hurricanes stop. When that happens, I don't know what to expect."

"There is still a lot that we don't understand," Ozias said.

"When the time comes, hopefully we will be in Sahael among the other tribes and will know what we need to know by then," Lyshyla said.

They spoke throughout the night, until Oxum entered breathlessly.

"Mother, Father, Educator Lyshyla," Oxum said. "A large black ship passed us moments ago. Oya and I thought there may have been Ennead soldiers on it. The massive vessel sailed on, completely ignoring our small wooden ship, but I thought you should know. It had the silver symbol of Captain Lynch on the port side."

"This is troubling," Lyshyla said. "They may have been coming from Neroppoli and making their way back toward the Ash Gates of Niolo."

"But why would a ship bearing Captain Lynch's symbol be coming from that direction?" Oadira asked, standing from the table. “Was it the *Nightingale*?” She remembered the ship from her time when she was a little girl. She could practically sense the presence of evil as the mysterious ship passed them by.

“When the time comes, we will be in Sahael among the other tribes to get that question answered,” Lyshyla said.

Oadira sat down and thought internally. Flashbacks of the Ennead and the Narsans from her time when she was a little girl trying to get on the ship with her mother’s help made the moment unreal.

“I remembered having to deactivate the only gate after I went through it for the last time to prevent the Narsans from entering the great library and destroying all of our history, everything, and everyone in Timbuktu,” Lyshyla said.

“There must be a reason why the Narsans want to destroy Timbuktu,” Oadira said.

“The Narsans wanted to sever us from our history by destroying the great library city of Timbuktu. Your ancient blood makes it so that all the knowledge in that library flows through your Ancient Bloodline. It has the potential to enlighten you all with unlimited knowledge,” Lyshyla said.

“The Narsans wanted to keep our bloodline dormant and ignorant to what our true history is; they want to whitewash our history in their own image,” Ozias added.

Lyshyla nodded. “Yes, and I felt it necessary to cut off all contact with Amit, even if it meant me and my bloodline would have to wait years until the time was right to make another trip to the great library city, the center of all knowledge. I hoped by know someone would have reactivated the gates, but Ogum confirmed that isn’t the case.”

“Timbuktu seems like a wonderful place,” Oadira said after Oxum had left. “What more can you tell us about the large library city?"

A broad smile filled Lyshyla's face as she sat back in her chair. Her eyes looked toward the wooden rafters above as if imagining something beautiful from her memory.

"Timbuktu is a place that the people of Sahael and Alkebulan would visit and learn about their tribes and the lands in which they lived," she began. "They did this to learn how to plant on their lands and learn how to make remedies to heal themselves by sending their medicine doctors to help their own people. When a new remedy was discovered, they would share it with the great library using Nalace journals to record and preserve the knowledge for all of the people."

"These Nalace journals sound fascinating," Ozias said. "I wish I could use one. A journal with unlimited pages? That sounds amazing."

"The Educators were sent out to live all over Aarde with Nalace journals," Lyshyla continued. "Those unlimited pages allowed them the ability to write down and research whatever they saw. The knowledge from them made their way into the books in the vast library of Timbuktu. These Educators wrote down all the secrets of Aarde. There were other places visited by the Educators of Timbuktu as well. These secrets were kept within the doctoral council of Timbuktu. They each had access to the secrets, but they may have all died or were hunted down and killed by the Narsans for reasons beyond my understanding."

Lyshyla stared off into space, as if she was speaking to herself rather than to the people in the room.

"The library city of Timbuktu is a place for all Black people from all nations to be educated properly. It's why the Narsan want to destroy them because they fear the education of Black people. As a result, they want to enslave and eradicate them entirely. As you know, the Narsans are a group of witan supremacists who want to rid Aarde of Black people entirely. They want to take all black contributions and make it seem as if they are their own."

"Timbuktu was a neutral place for all races. I'm sure something must have changed all of that," Oadira said as she took a bite of what remained of the dried fruit.

"As time went on, we had multiple visits from the Narsans, none from the Rysallians," Lyshyla said. "Nothing was forbidden. We even had visits from Lord Commander Natas when---"

"Lord Commander Natas himself visited Timbuktu?" Oadira interrupted.

"Yes. Keep in mind, Timbuktu was open and, as you said, neutral to all. It wasn't a shock someone like Natas would come there to study. Lord Commander Natas followed the rules of the library."

Oadira squeezed the dried fruit between her thumb and finger. "This is the same Lord Commander Natas that infiltrated and invaded Sahael—you taught him? You armed him with knowledge that he's now using against Aarde?"

A deep breath filled Lyshyla's chest. "At the time, none of us knew. He appeared as the first ever Black Narsan, which was unheard of and not possible, which intrigued us as well. Remember, Timbuktu is about knowledge, not war or threats or betrayal. It was…*is*…an innocent place of learning. No one was ever seen as a threat, not even Natas."

"That's interesting," Oadira replied.

"We saw Natas' arrival as an opportunity to learn more about him and his higher realm. I met Lord Commander Natas in passing. He is dangerous, but at the time, he appeared innocent. He was just a Black man from Narsa who was confused and wanted to prove his parents wrong and that he could make a difference. I didn't realize his parents were Ishtar and Obatala. Natas then advocated for all witan westerners to be allowed in Timbuktu; we didn't object. After all, Timbuktu was for everyone."

"You educated our enemies," Ozias said, shaking his head.

"We didn't know they were enemies," Lyshyla defended, voice firm. "We barely understood what enemies were, or that anyone would ever seek the destruction of other people. Again, we were innocent. Lord Commander Natas convinced the doctoral council that he was in great pain, explaining that his outward appearance was changing from that of a Black man to a witan, which allowed him to stay longer than expected in Timbuktu."

"Wow, you just let him plot and plan your own demise," Ozias said in a sarcastic tone.

Lyshyla leaned forward and pointed at Oadira. "This is why I don't speak of this with anyone. You see things from the perspective of darkness, but we had no such viewpoint. Our understanding was of light and trust, not death and darkness. Lord Commander Natas ventured throughout the library city of Timbuktu, learning about each individual tribe, lineage, and bloodline sent down to Aarde."

"That explains how Lord Commander Natas knew all that there was to know about the tribes," Oadira said.

"Yes," Lyshyla said, hand dropping to the table. "Natas learned about Nzingha and each of his four keys that were placed in three of the four realms in eastern Aarde. He learned through the White Darkness that Nzingha's forth key was placed in the crypts of Sahael, about Nabopollassar, Nebuchadnezzar, Nzingha, Nebiriau, Nectanebo; the role of the Ogdoad lineage that was split into two; the Amun and the Keni bloodlines; and the role Egyptus had in helping to conceal Nzingha's obsidian key in the crypts of Sahael."

"All of the bracelets, rings, gates, realms—it's all from the ancient Kemites to help us get to Sahael?" Oadira asked. "These Kemites created everything, and why are they not here using that technology to help us get back to Sahael? Nabopollassar and his four seals, Nebuchadnezzar and his four portals, and Nzingha and his four keys."

"Something must have happened to all of them," Ozias said.

Lyshyla tapped her finger against the wooden table. "They were in Sahael when Khartoum Palace was invaded from within. The four Pharaohs were scattered and lost after their fathers and mothers were killed."

"There must be a reason why Natas was learning about these Kemite leaders and artifacts," Oadira said. "The Lord Commander sent Captain Lynch to retrieve Nzingha's sapphire key for a reason. Finding out that reason is crucial to understanding what it is he has planned."

"Apart from what you already know, Nzingha's keys were built to keep darkness from entering Aarde. If all four keys were collected, they would provide the ability to remove Nabopollassar's four seals on each of Nullify's gates in the four realms. Natas spent a lot of time learning about the four realms created by Nier, Neros, Nethal, and Naharis in Aarde. Natas became enamored with Naharis's realm; learning that his dominion had control over death as the only realm connected to outer darkness. If Lord Commander Natas learned anything specific, he kept it to himself."

"Perhaps Nalace's Encyclopedias, books, journals, and articles in Timbuktu can provide us more insight," Oadira said.

A knock was heard on their door, interrupting them as they spoke. Ora the Ouadane Navigator poked her head in with a nod.

"My king and queen," she said. "Educator Lyshyla. The currents have intensified. While it is dark, we see the fogs becoming thicker. My years on the ocean are telling me we are approaching land."

As morning dawned, the thick fog gave way enough to see land close by.

"The island of Amit," Ora whispered to Oadira. "It is said to be surrounded by an impenetrable rock wall that no one can climb."

Over the next hour they floated closer until they made out a solid rock structure with no openings, jutting from the water like a giant wall one hundred feet high. It was made of hardened molten rock. As they traveled around the perimeter of the island, never finding any gates or gaps, they spotted other ships patrolling its outer molten rock area. They too were looking for an opening that could lead into the island.

"How did they get here?" Oadira asked, pointing at one vessel a mile away, firing cannons on the impenetrable barrier.

"Most likely on the Emperor and Empress' ocean current, as we did," Ora replied.

"We need to avoid being spotted by the ships firing on Amit," Lyshyla warned as a blast of cannon fire echoed through the fog. "Let's keep sailing and hide in the mist as best we can."

Another hour passed and they came upon a section of wall inscribed with symbols Oadira had never seen before. She stared at them silently as they drifted past.

"Oadira," Lyshyla shouted suddenly. "Your tattoos are lighting up, which means you're seeing something that only you and your family can see."

Just then, the four boys, Oshún, Oxum, Oya, and Onika ran up from below deck, tattoos glowing on their muscular arms and shoulders.

"Mother, Father!" Onika shouted. "What's going on?"

"All of you," Lyshyla advised. "Blink twice to activate your cerulean eyes, and you'll be able to see what you need. This is for the royal bloodline to see."

Oadira, Ozias, and their boys, did as instructed and scanned the mountainous area.

"Because your eyes are lit, you will see what most eyes are unable to see," Lyshyla said.

"Boys, look," Ozias said, pointing.

Oadira focused, seeing a glowing symbol of the Orishan coat of arms; the symbol of Ankh with a water dragon's head in the open space of the symbol. Word flared beneath it that Oadira understood from her years of studying ancient bloodline texts.

"Follow the current, and it will bring us in contact with the mountain," Oadira ordered. She pointed to the navigator at the helm. "Remove your hand from the wheel. Let the water take us where it wants to go."

The navigators turned into the current and released the steering wheel. It spun quickly as the water swung the ship away from the wall and then swiftly back again. The fog lifted and there in the ocean before them was a mountain of rock jutting from the waves.

"We're going to crash into the structure," one of Ogum's crewmen said.

"We need to jump ship and swim under this large mountain if we are wanting to make it into the city of Timbuktu," Oadira shouted. "It's the only way we're going to get inside of this mountain. Trust the signs! Trust the ocean!"

"What about those of us who can't breathe under water?" Ora asked, looking at the mountain as it quickly approached.

"Steer the boat away!" Ozias ordered. "If we get inside, we will find a way for you to enter. I promise! Stay in this area. We'll figure something out!"

Ora nodded and grabbed the wheel to steer the ship to safety just as the royal family and Lyshyla jumped into the ocean, swimming deep into the depths of the waters, reaching the bottom of the Nambissian floor.

Follow me, Oadira said telepathically, taking the lead. They swam under the rocks, quickly entering a dark area of opaque water. Their tattoos continued glowing though, shedding light all around them. As they dove deeper, breathing freely of the water, Oadira saw light ahead. There on a polished section of rock glowed a single Nairo gate built into the wall of the mountain. The gate activated as Oadira's cerulean eyes interacted with the waters. The entrance became transparent as the symbol of the Marula Tree appeared and then faded.

Let's enter, Oadira said.

They immediately swam through the Nairo gate, emerging on the other side of the mountainous structure. Light filtered through the water above, reflecting off fish flitting through the current.

We can swim up to the surface. I see a docking platform, Oadira said to everyone.

Breaking the surface, Oadira breathed the warm air. They climbed onto the docking platform and looked around at the wall to their left and a beach to their right. Beyond the sand weaved a stone path leading into a jungle of vibrant green.

"Follow me," Lyshyla said, squeezing water from her long

hair. " I know this place. We can get to Timbuktu from here. This cobblestone road will take us to the inner forest of Timbuktu."

The royal family followed Lyshyla into the forest. The heat was stifling as insects buzzed around them and strange sounds echoed from beyond the trees.

"How will we get the boat through the wall?" Oxum asked as he swatted at a mosquito. "Ora and Yasuké have to help us with the gates, right?"

"Once we're in the city," Lyshyla said as she continued walking, "we'll have someone open one of the hidden wall gates. As long as they stay in the area of the mountain, we should be able to find them easily."

After an hour of walking, Oadira, Ozias, Lyshyla, and the boys arrived in the great city of Timbuktu. The entire city was designed as a library located in the center of the mountainous island of Amit in the Nambissian Sea. Thick Marula Trees surrounded buildings of white stone, polished, and shining in the early afternoon sun. Lakes, rivers, streams, and large fluffy clouds acted as a frame to what Oadira could only describe as the most regal city she had ever seen. Even the towers of Neith in Nier's Realm could not compare.

Lyshyla led the group through a multitude of large buildings, the beautiful city that housed the knowledge of Aarde. They walked through the metropolis, seeing buildings everywhere.

But no people.

Their footsteps echoed as they walked. Birds chirped overhead, but otherwise Timbuktu was a silent tomb of stoic beauty.

"Where is everybody?" Onika asked as they passed a ten-foot-tall marble statue of a man in robes holding a large book.

"I do not know," Lyshyla answered. She looked around

constantly as if someone would jump out at them. “The city was evacuated 50 years ago when Natas attacked Sahael. I was there. But I never guessed it would remain empty all this time.”

They passed another statue, this one of a woman holding scrolls of knowledge over her head. A bird’s nest had been constructed on the top of her head.

“Timbuktu historically is the most important educational city in Aarde for the four kingdoms, the four realms, Alkebulan, Aarde, Egyptus, and the other floating islands,” Lyshyla continued. “This whole city is one giant library, with connecting buildings above and below the surface.”

“So, is everyone reading underground somewhere?” Oshún asked with a chuckle.

Oadira looked at Lyshyla, who had stopped next to a painted mural of men and women sitting in a grassy meadow while an orator taught a lesson.

“Lyshyla, are you okay?” she asked.

“I need some time to myself; My stomach is knotting up,” Lyshyla, voice breaking with emotion.

“Are you okay?” Oadira asked again.

“I’m all right.” Lyshyla replied. “I taught many students, especially Lord Commander Natas and the Narsans who insisted on knowing everything about the Ancient Order and the library of the ancients. They were extremely good students, eager to learn. I just need a moment to…think and feel.”

Lyshyla sat down in the silent city and wept for a few minutes. Oadira looked around, understanding Lyshyla’s pain, but only to a point. Lyshyla was far older than Oadira, though she didn’t look it. The Educator had seen and experienced far more than Oadira could understand. Much like Oadira’s memories of her mistakes not fighting back as a youth on the Lalaurie Estate still weighed heavy in her memory, so too much Lyshyla's of her time here in Timbuktu.

And now, the city Lyshyla had always talked so much about with its innocent and knowledge-loving people, sat completely empty and deserted. It would be like returning to your home after a long absence and expecting your family to be there waiting but finding only dust and memories in their place.

Eventually, Lyshyla recovered and again led them past ornate buildings all silent and lifeless.

"We've arrived at the Royal Sahaelian library," Lyshyla said as they approached a large, towering brass building with pillars and sculptures adorning the front. The shiny edifice gleamed proudly in the sun, lighting up the entire area. "The library has one hundred floors," Lyshyla said, pointing up at the massive structure. "Twenty-five levels each belong to one of the four major bloodlines. The top level of the one hundredth floor is connected by the Nairohenge Gates, linking the library to the four kingdoms in Sahael to Khartoum Palace, the realms, and the other floating islands."

"The doors seem to be sealed shut," Oadira said, pointing at the carved silver doors and a layer of melted metal fusing them together. "How do we get inside? I also see the Sahaelian image of the Marula Tree that needs to be activated allowing us entry."

"This library is made from Orichalcum. The ancients must have built it," Ozias said.

Oadira touched the symbol of the Marula Tree with her fingers. The engraving glowed aquamarine and allowing the royal family to automatically open the doors. They slid back and to the sides, scrapping against the tile ground and echoing in the space beyond.

"After you," Oadira said to Lyshyla, motioning for the

Educator to lead the way.

While inside the royal library, they could see the four great halls with symbols at the top of each entryway. Light streamed in from open shafts or windows hundreds of feet above. It was hard to see exactly how the light entered, but the library was surprisingly bright and inviting. Each of the great halls were shielded with sapphire, emerald, hematite, and turquoise, shielding fields preventing the royal family from entering the other educational areas of the imperial library.

Oadira walked through Nilor's forcefield, deactivating it and allowing Lyshyla to move through the Orishan wing freely.

"Is it safe to assume Lord Commander Natas and the Narsans spent a lot of time in this library?" Oadira asked, looking up at bookshelves that towered over even her tallest son, each housing thousands of volumes.

"Natas and the Narsans wanted to understand the powers of the four blooded families," Lyshyla answered. "I felt because Lord Commander Natas was in Timbuktu and under the code of conduct and bound by the Nairobi laws of innocence, it was okay to teach him and the Narsans."

"It just doesn't make sense that you'd teach a witan that could use whatever is taught against Black people," Ozias said, shaking his head. "Did that thought ever occur in your intelligent brains?"

Lyshyla sat down in front of the Orishan chamber hall to gather her thoughts.

"No one is born wicked," Lyshyla said. "No race is inherently evil. Once evil is taught and then mixed with power dynamics, it can grow and fester and infect. Natas is a being of power and hate. He has used it against our people all across Aarde, but he just as easily could have infected us with his hate and used it against witans. Perhaps that would have been even worse, since we would have become the evil force that preys on the weak."

She blew dust from a small table next to her, revealing a map of all Aarde. It was intricate and beautifully designed.

"This knowledge is available to everyone in Timbuktu," Lyshyla continued. "All the people of Aarde have a right to be informed and educated, despite how they might turn around and use the information for personal good, or evil gains. It's my job as an Educator to teach, not to judge. That's how it will always be in Timbuktu. Natas continued to ask where the four seals were located. I answered and explained to him they were created by Nabopollassar, one of the ancient Kemites, to seal away the hosts who were cast out of Andalusia by Ishtar and Obatala. I told him about Nebuchadnezzar and his four portals that were created in each of the four realms inside of Nullify's gates. Natas was intrigued and captivated by all this information. Over time, he started putting things together in his head."

Lyshyla paused to catch her breath. "Lord Commander Natas and the Narsans wanted to understand each of the four realms and what impact they had on Aarde. Lord Natas learned that the four realms were adjacent to each other." She pointed at the map carved on the table next to her. "If you are looking down at this map, you will see that the east is at the top with the north to the right, south to the left, and at the bottom, the west. Natas learned that the Yoruban's resided in eastern Aarde. The Hausan's resided in western Aarde and that Naharis's realm, home of the Demir, was on the left side of a map. Natas learned about the geography of where each realm was located and wanted to learn more about Sahael and the Ancient Order. I taught Natas that there were twelve tribes of the Ancient Order. He took the time to learn about all twelve but focused mainly on the tribes of the Chosen Bloodline. When Natas asked about death among the chosen order, I explained that death did not apply to the Chosen Bloodlines or to death in general in which the three realms had no control."

Lyshyla brushed what little dust remained on the map.

"Lord Commander Natas, according to Nalace's journal, was able to replicate and get a hold of Nzingha's blueprints to create a copy of his onyx key. The White Darkness revealed the secrets of the ancients and where Nzinga's obsidian key was located after Natas replicated the onyx key, he placed it inside of Nectanebo's key slot. The White Darkness revealed the location of Nzingha's obsidian key buried in Necrosis's chamber in Khartoum Palace; only the four kings and queens of Sahael knew of its location. Natas learned that the four realms chose Naharis's realm as the stewards over the dead."

"That's an odd place to hide Nzingha's obsidian key," Ozias said.

"It was traded with Sahael and Egyptus in exchange for bringing Morrighan and Sekhmet of the cursed Demirrians back to Sahael in exchange for restoring the eyesight of their baby girl, Damisiah, with two turquoise stones. They were cursed because Morrighan of Ketta and Sekhmet of Egypt merged bloodlines. As a result, their people, children, and bloodline were cursed with albino skin; they are known as the Black albinos." Lyshyla said.

"I'm sure Lord Commander Natas had a reason for doing all of this. It doesn't make sense," Oadira said.

A sadness pulled down at the edges of Lyshyla's mouth. "Lord Commander Natas learned that with Nzingha's obsidian key, he could help save every Aardian and get them back to the presence of the divines, giving them one path to choose and no other options."

"Lord Commander Natas just wanted a way to save people," Ozias said.

"Isn't that a good thing?" Oxum replied. "All we've ever

heard is how evil Natas is, but if his plan was to save everyone so we could return to Andalusia, wouldn't that be a plan worth accepting?"

Lyshyla's eyes narrowed. "Perhaps Natas truly did want to bring everyone back....but if you ask me, Natas simply wanted the glory of doing so. His motivations were always selfish. He has the right to find any information in Timbuktu that could possibly help. Lord Natas wanted to know personally if bodiless spirits could enter dead bodies that were no longer housing an Aardian soul. I explained to him that the realms and laws would not apply to them since the dead can't be judged, meaning they could go unchecked and unchallenged, doing whatever they wanted on Aarde."

"You created Lord Commander Natas," Ozias said candidly, without judgement. "You educated him, motivated him, and armed him with all he needed to kill and enslave all the Black people in Aarde."

A tear trickled down Lyshyla's face, but she made no attempt to wipe it away. "I did, and others. He was such an amazing pupil. We loved him, truly. When Lord Natas knew he could save every Andalusian and get them all back to the sacred afterlife, I never saw him again until the invasion of Sahael and the destruction of Khartoum Palace. I asked him how, but Natas refused to tell me. He said he had found a way to save everyone and prove his mother and father wrong. Natas wanted to prove he could save everyone, including the dead. Now that we are here in Timbuktu, you have all the resources to fact-check all that I told you and will tell you while we are here. The first thing I'd like you to do is to learn more about the Andalusian bloodline; it's crucial to your history as a people, family, and bloodline. Not only is your history special, but it's also sacred and now forbidden from others to learn."

"We still don't know what Natas is up to in the meantime,"

Oadira said. "Getting to Sahael is still the priority. We are here now and learning all that we can, may provide us clues that could help as we get closer to Sahael. First, we need to get the ship inside the walls so that Ora the Ouadane Navigator and Yasuké the Medjay Gate Guardian can help activate the Nairohenge Gates."

"There's nobody here to ask how to do that," Oya replied, voice echoing through the chamber. "We promised Ogum we would protect his wife, Ora. We can't leave her and Yasuké out there with those other ships."

"I have an idea," Lyshyla said. "Let us go back to the beach. I remember a latch in that area that can open a breach in the wall. If Ora and Yasuké stayed near the mountain as instructed, we should be able to get them in."

After a long trek back to the beach, Lyshyla located a brass handle attached to a set of gears that ran under an orichalcum platform. From the docking stage, Lyshyla moved the mechanism from down to up. Waves churned as the wall opened. Fog poured in. After a few minutes, Ogum's ship came into view.

But it wasn't alone.

One of the ships they had seen firing their cannons on the wall earlier in the day was following the wake of Ogum's craft. A flash of fire burst from cannons before the sound reached the beach.

"They're firing on Ora and Yasuké!" Oadira shouted.

"We can't let that ship enter Timbuktu!" Ozias yelled.

"Pull the mechanism down, Lyshyla," Oadira ordered. "Close the wall!"

""Our ship is too close!" Lyshyla said. "It will be crushed if we close the breach."

"There must be something we can do to get the ship

inside," Oadira said.

More cannons fired. Both ships approached quickly.

"There is something we can do," Lyshyla yelled. "We can use the ship slide to get them in," Lyshyla said.

"How is that even possible?" Ozias asked.

"Inside of this mechanism is a button. By pressing the button, a sinkhole will be created, making the other ships think that Ogum's ship is being destroyed. It's a security measure by the Amit's defenses. This'll bring Ogum's ship here to the docking port." Lyshyla pointed to the location of where the ship would be after moving through the sinkhole.

"Okay, do it," Oadira said.

Lyshyla pulled the lever down, closing the opening and creating a sinkhole that allowed the ship to sink and slide into the Amit covertly. At the same time, the swirling water pushed the invading ship beyond the breach so it could be safely closed again. Ogum's crew was able to dock and depart the ship.

"We wondered if you would find us a way inside," Ora said as she jumped onto the beach from the gangplank.

"We are sorry for the delay," Oadira smiled. "We can take you to the city, but there is no one there."

"No people at all?" Yasuké asked.

"None," Lyshyla confirmed. "It seems as though no one ever came back once the threat of Natas had manifested. Let us return to the city for the night. There are many fruit trees in the groves that will give us food. Let us learn what we can, and perhaps discover why no one stayed behind to guard this sacred land."

Over the next few days, Lyshyla, the children, Ozias, and Oadira started roaming and looking around the Orishan royal library. They picked fruit and found several overgrown gardens that still had plenty of wild vegetables. They took turns foraging and reading, trying to discover whatever they could. Ora and Yasuké looked around the rest of the library for anything on the Nairohenge Gates.

Occasionally cannon fire could be heard as the ships that had found their way to the island on The Emperor and Empress' current continued trying to get beyond the outer wall. The currents had died down once Oadira and the family had arrived, meaning the ships had no way of sailing away. They would eventually starve, but they could not be allowed to enter Timbuktu. It was too big of a risk.

"After going through the library," Oadira said to Lyshyla as she sat next to her in a reading area of the Orishan library wing. "Ozias and I stumbled on the origins of our bloodlines. We learned that half of our lineage was separated into four separate bloodlines on my side."

Lyshyla nodded. "The Andalusian ancestry separated into four bloodlines that emanated directly from Ishtar and Obatala. They were the Ara Orun, people derived from Andalusia. They came from the city of Anda, yet they no longer reside there. The Orishan's, Yoruba, Hausa, and Demirrians are Irunmole, Aarde's first racially mixed inhabitants, and are now sacred beings dwelling in Aarde. They were kings, cultural heroes and heroines, warriors, and founders of cities, who had a major influence over the lives of their people and are recognized in Orishan society for their contributions to culture and social life."

"I learned that in Orishan tradition, individuals were able to establish control over a natural force that created a bond of interdependence with it, attracting its beneficent action toward themselves and their people while sending its destructive aspects onto their enemies," Oadira explained. "To achieve this degree of control and interdependence, the Orishans made offerings and sacrifices. They later disappeared often, and according to tradition, in a remarkable manner, by sinking into the waters and forming homes below the lake of Sahael where they built Sahaedron, the underwater realm. However, during Natas's invasion, hundreds, and thousands of Orishan's, Yoruban's, Demirrians, and Hausan's were killed, enslaved, uprooted, and transported to the outer provinces of the eastern lands of Aarde. The responsibility of the Orishan's fell to Obatala's descendants to transmit their knowledge to subsequent generations, through objects and secrets which they can interact with the Watchers of the four realms."

"Yes," Lyshyla said, pulling a book from the table next to her and opening its pages. "Lord Commander Natas learned that each Orishan had specific occupations, skills, and preferences; no diseases nor problems; many capabilities; and little misfortune. They were a perfect and peaceful culture. Natas heard what he needed to hear, understanding that the Orishan's were the guardians and explicators of their own destiny. Natas saw them as a threat to his indoctrination process. He didn't want the Alkebulan people to turn to the Orishans for help, aid, and advice to save them. It was believed that the Chosen Bloodlines were completely eradicated by Natas."

Ozias approached and kissed Oadira on the cheek. "What are you two discussing? More history and such?"

"Always, my love," Oadira smiled, snuggling against his neck. "We're talking about what you and I found out about the Orishans."

"Well, in that case," Ozias chuckled. "I found a few interesting tidbits. The Yoruban's, the Demirrians, and the Hausan's were also descendants sent down to Aarde by Ishtar and Obatala. They were united by geography, history, religion, and most importantly, language. They all spoke Sahaelian. When all four tribes come together, they share the common tongue of the ancients. The surrounding countries spoke various languages, but the Sahaelians could speak every language of the Alkebulans and Aardians. A gift that only they could use when all Sahael was back in balance and unified as one in Alkebulan. With all this information, Natas armed himself to do all that he wanted. Natas knew what he was doing from the start."

"During the Narsan invasion, many of the Yoruban people were forcibly taken out of their homelands," Lyshyla agreed. "The Demirrians were enslaved in their own realm. I heard that they were slaughtered, their numbers dwindled and so did their lands. The western powers of Aarde, Narsans, Triennium, Dales, the T.I.M., divided up the continent of Alkebulan into different pieces and created new countries and languages. This caused division and that is why Ishtar and Obatala wanted to unite the twelve bloodlines, to unite the people and end the suffering of the Alkebulans. The Hausan's suffered the same treatment as the Orishan's and the Yoruban's. The only difference is they were placed in large bird cages and shipped out to the mountainous regions of Nuberia. Lord Commander Natas used his forces to transport them up the large mountains. The abandoned people were left alone in cages until they eventually starved to death."

"How terrible," Ozias said. He sat down next to Lyshyla. "Once the Chosen Bloodlines were scattered, they were left alone to fend for themselves. From what I've read, they are known as the givers of life who provide life to all in the realms and throughout Aarde. It's clear that Lord Commander Natas knew everything he wanted to know about the four Chosen Bloodlines and the realms."

"I learned more about the Watchers as I read through their history," Oadira explained. "They were Ishtar and Obatala's closest and most loyal subjects, who sacrificed their position and left Ishtar and Obatala to come down to Aarde to help be the Chosen Bloodlines. They consisted of the bloodline of giants known as the Nephilim, giants who stood over twelve feet tall and were full of intelligence. They helped with the building of the first pyramids in Egyptus with the Lysinnians. They were also a part of the Chosen Bloodlines when their bloodline merged with the Negralli bloodline. Their merging created the Orishan bloodline, which was the lineage created when my mother and father were married."

Ozias placed his hand on his wife's shoulder. "Since Lord Commander Natas was interested in death and spirits, I found information on Neros's realm referred to as the spirit realm or the realm of souls. When an Aardian loses their life, their spirit leaves the body and travels east toward the Gates of Negrunde while the body lies lifeless. The spirit travels for weeks, days, even months until it reaches the Negrundian Gates. When the spirit reaches the realm, the empress and emperor of the realm open their gates with Nzingha's emerald key, allowing them to pass through Nebuchadnezzar's portal, Nabopollassar's seal, on Nullify's gate."

"Then the spirit is met by the Negrundian guardians who bring that spirit down the halls to be judged by the emperor and empress," Oadira continued. "The rulers send the spirit into one of two places after its initial judgment, spiritual paradise or spiritual prison, until the Nethanites escort them to one of the three realms of glory. The responsibility of the eastern Watchers is that they are the sworn protectors of Alkebulan life. It is their responsibility to help and protect them against their enemies no matter the severity of their transgressions."

"Your family is destined to do things in Aarde that I cannot even fathom," Lyshyla said, rubbing her forehead. "They know not what lies before them. The bloodline you all share is in some ways as much a curse as it is a blessing with the responsibilities and expectations that come along with it. But before it gets better, it's going to get worse. In this case, it's just never going to get better; they're going to be hunted for the rest of their eternal lives. Their children and their children's children will be hunted for the rest of their eternal lives, even when we get to Sahael, change is coming. I just cannot imagine the obstacles they're going to face as young Black boys growing into men in a whitewashed version of Aarde."

Ozias stretched his back. "I fear for Aarde, but my heart hurts even more for the future of my children. Eventually, they'll leave my sight. They'll have to learn to navigate this world. It scares me that Aarde will remove them from under my watchful eyes. But until that time comes, I'll continue to enjoy their presence."

"I understand, Ozias," Lyshyla said, placing her hand on his shoulder. "That is something you will have to learn to cope with. The hope is that Oadira and you have taught your sons how to code switch in Aarde, a skill they'll have to master before they get to Sahael."

Lyshyla, Oadira, and Ozias continued their conversation on their way to the sleeping quarters. They walked through the Orishan hallways to their gorgeous sleeping quarters, resembling their quarters in Nier's realm.

"I was reading and recognized that there were five or six tribes that were highly favored in Aarde that Ishtar and Obatala blessed," Oadira said. "They were the only four tribes Obatala selected and blessed with the blood of the ancients. The other two tribes were the Lysinnians, my tribe, and the Rysallians. The Lysinnians were blessed with infinite knowledge and were visited by Ishtar and Obatala to help educate the Chosen Bloodlines and all the other inhabitants of Aarde. It was our duty to follow the precepts that were laid out before us. When Sahael was infiltrated from within, all my people were sent to Inheritance and have remained there safely, until the initial gathering can be completed. The gathering of the Sahaelian bloodlines never took place. The Rysallians headed out west, feeling cheated and disrespected because they hadn't received any gifts from the divines."

"They inherited a disposition for violence that Lord Commander Natas tapped into using for his own means," Lyshyla explained. "They are the reason the initial gathering never took place. The sacred six tribes never gathered. Because of this, there was a great dispersion amongst the six tribes that sent them all over Aarde. After Sahael was settled by the Kemites, they were instructed to reach out to the Rysallians, who needed the guidance of the other five tribes."

After Lyshyla left, Ozias blew out the candles and they went to sleep. Oadira couldn't rest, however. The constant bombardment from the ships hitting the mountain kept her awake. She got up and noticed Lyshyla wasn't in her sleeping quarters, so she wandered down to the library to see what she was doing. Oadira wandered the library, feeling Lyshyla's frustrated emotions. They grew stronger as she approached the main staircase that spiraled upward to the top floor. Oadira had only taken the long trek once, since it took over an hour to climb the stairs to the top floor, but she felt compelled to do so now.

She climbed through the night, making her way to the Orishan library where the Nairohenge Gates were located. Lyshyla's emotions grew stronger with each passing minute. Eventually Oadira reached the top floor and observed Lyshyla pouring over books and maps. Ora and Yasuké assumed their rightful places on the sides of the gate doors. The Nairohenge Gates had risen from the ground when Oadira arrived, unlocking the doors to enter the library.

"What's going on?" Oadira asked.

"We found the passages and codewords to access the gates," Ora smiled as light flowed from the stones of the gateway.

"With the Nairohenge Gates only able to make transport possible to Nier's realm and back," Lyshyla said, "traveling back to Sahael is still a challenge. I still need to find out where the lost tribes were scattered over Aarde during the first gathering."

Oadira ran over to where Lyshyla sat with the books. "The Nairohenge Gates are operational! Is it possible to determine where this gate will take us?"

"No," Lyshyla said with frustration in her voice. "They will only take you to Nier's realm and back. They still must be reactivated from different locations all over Aarde. There is great risk or death traveling through unstable energy from only one source. It would be a one-way trip to a hostile place. Maybe that would allow us to get closer to Sahael, if you're willing to take the risk."

"I believe it's a risk worth taking. We have the means to take care of ourselves if we must. It's time to wake everyone and get going," Oadira said.

CHAPTER VIII

THE CHOSEN BASTARDS

Timbuktu, The United DIM-TIM Lands, The Society of Secrets

Oadira descended the spiral; staircase far more quickly than she had climbed it, hurrying to her room to wake Ozias, who helped her wake up the princes. The family got ready as quickly as possible, walking up thousands of stairs to the top, following Oadira and Ozias. It was morning by the time they reached the top of the library. The sun rose over the island and Oadira could see the wall in the distance, as well as the ocean stretching on endlessly beyond.

Lyshyla met them as they arrived on the top floor of the Sahaelian library, where the Nairohenge Gates were located. The royal family was ordered to stand in the center of the Nairohenge Gates and the single Nairo gates. They observed Ora and Yasuké as they performed their artes.

"Do we know where this gate will take us?" Ozias asked.

"Yes," Lyshyla confirmed. "Ora of the Ouadane Navigators and Yasuké of the Medjay Gate Guardians are here to help us get to where we need to go. Once we are through the gates, they'll be able to travel back to Nier's realm, where they're needed to help assist Sahael. They must keep the waters in the north on their currents, restoring life to the oceans of Aarde. I'll be bringing maps with us in my backpack to help us on our journey."

Ora took a knee, allowing Lyshyla to look at the elaborate designs on the top of her head. Yasuké the Medjay Gate Guardian stood on the left side of the gate and knew which path to take upon entering the door through the single Nairohenge Gate. Yasuké watched over Ora, the wife of Ogum of the Ouadane, with great care. They were inseparable and bonded to each other forever. They both had brown-colored eyes with specks of blue, representing tribes that were lost and scattered in Aarde.

"Without every gate operational, how confident are you that the Navigator will get us to Sahael?" Ozias asked. "What do we do if something happens that is beyond our control?"

"Whatever we have to," Lyshyla said with a stern voice.

"Agreed," Oadira replied.

"Everyone, hold hands as we enter through Nairohenge," Lyshyla suggested.

The lines on Ora's head lit up in cerulean, as did her eyes due to the sapphire specks in her brown irises. On the top of Ora's head, an energy moved down the back of her neck, forming a map on Ora's back, revealing itself to Yasuké, so he could show the others where they were going.

The royal family and Lyshyla entered through one of the Nairohenge Gate doors, walking into a warm paradise. Ora the Navigator walked in front of Yasuké, who looked at the map on her back as Lyshyla and the royal family followed behind her. They walked through a three-hundred-foot-wide labyrinth bridge connected to the other side of the Nairohenge Gate. Paths shot off in all directions. Yasuké would take a left turn, then a right, following the map on Ora's back and leading them through the maze. The Nairobridge had running water on both sides and radiant sunlight with a surrounding forest full of Marula Trees providing a place of solace and comfort.

"I can see why the Navigators are important. Without them you'd get lost and die," Oya said as he walked quickly next to his mother.

"So, if anyone were to deviate off the course of the bridge, they could be stuck here forever?" Oadira asked.

"Worse," Lyshyla said as Yasuké took another left in the maze. "Hidden inside these forests are wraiths who capture those lost on the bridge or the In-between. They are killed instantly. The bodies are sent to Naharis's realm and the spirits are kicked out to roam Aarde freely, without purpose, as vengeful ghosts; upset that they've been left alone to wander aimlessly, waiting to ascend, descend, or transcend."

"I understand the need to have Navigators and Guardians as escorts," Ozias replied. "I thought it was just a matter of opening the gateway, not following the right path sequence on the bridge too. Amazing."

The royal family and Lyshyla made it to the other side of the Nairostone Gate, entering through it. Ora and Yasuké remained on the Nairobridge in the In-between, traveling back through the Nairobridge to the Nairohenge Gate on their way back to Nier's realm.

"Farewell," the two guides waved. "Return to Sahael and right these wrongs!"

"Thank you, Ora!" Oadira cried. "Thank you Yasuké! We will find our way back because of your aid. Journey well back to Nier's Realm."

Passing through the final energy barrier, the group stepped foot in an open land of green grass, blown by a warm wind from the south. The sun shone high in the sky, slowly making its way toward evening. White stones surrounded them in broken chunks as big as a man. A wall stood before them, ancient and crumbling, but still tall and impenetrable. It arched slightly as if a massive circle, similar to the wall that surrounded the island of Amit.

"Where are we? Are we lost?" Oadira asked.

"I don't know, Let's look around," Lyshyla suggested.

"There's nothing but open land everywhere," Ozias said.

Lyshyla picked up a few of the smaller white stones and examined them. She climbed on a larger boulder and looked all around.

"We are at the wall of TRIM, I believe," Lyshyla said, looking off into the distant grasslands. "A wall was built within the mountains of the D.I.M.–T.I.M. Lands. We are in the D.I.M. Nations. They always keep the walls clean and white so that when the sun reflects off them, you won't be able to find your bearings. The two nations believe in 'separate but equal,' although some in the T.I.M. Nations have increasingly felt different about it. The Black people in the D.I.M. Nations were prospering more than they should compared to the witans."

Lyshyla surveyed the surrounding area and pulled a few maps from her leather backpack. "There are three separate countries that make up the D.I.M. Nations consisting of the Dogon, Immi, and Myti," Lyshyla said without lifting her eyes from her map. She turned to Oadira and Ozias. "The Narsans learned the Jericho method, circling the continent seven times, bringing down the walls of TRIM down, allowing them the ability to travel over the mountains and into Black lands. This allowed the Narsans and the Ennead to invade and take control of their governments using phylacteries to help control their minds."

"That's terrible! They were brainwashed to serve," Oadira

said.

"It happened quickly," Lyshyla explained."With that type of control, the Trinity increased their ranks with thousands of people from D.I.M. Nations to help invade and take control of Alkebulan. Those who chose not to join the Trinity made the personal choice of committing suicide on the inside, feeling numb and mindless, converting to the servants of the dead. They became the Nethanites, serving the beings taught to hear the dead sing. It's the name the Narsan government branded them, after they choose to take part in the Nauthian gospel as full converts."

"It seems like they just rolled over and took it on the chin," Ozias said.

Lyshyla nodded. "Consequently, they had to fight against those who had their minds influenced by the Narsan government and its officials. Primarily because they wanted to see death. They loved the way they would feel around death, so they were sent somewhere to be around death for the rest of their days. The remnants of the D.I.M Nations are fragile people, and we need to find out how they can help us or us them."

"We need to determine what's going on," Ozias said. "If the Narsans took over these lands, are they still in control? I have no desire to see my sons captured by servants of Natas."

"Agreed," Oadira said.

Climbing up another of the large stones, Lyshyla once again examined the large barrier closely. "Climbing over this wall needs to be avoided at all costs to make sure Narsan forces don't find us and enslave us. Looking for an opening to avoid having to climb is our best hope to stay hidden."

Oadira nodded and moved ahead of the group, keeping her eyes peeled for an access point. After walking several hours, Oadira eventually spotted an opening of the crumbled structure.

Oadira looked back at the group, whistling to get their attention.

"I found an opening that will allow us to get through undetected and avoid any unwanted eyes," she said.

"The skies are darkening," Lyshyla said. The sun had long ago set behind the wall. "Shelter is our main priority to avoid the Nethani who are worshippers of the dead. When they find living Black albinos at night, they confiscate and take them underground to Necropolis. Then they offer them up as sacrifices, allowing their bodies to be taken through Nebuchadnezzar's portal by the Nethanites. These Nethani are rejected and cursed Aardians that weren't allowed to die and now must eternally live in damnation. Their bodies rot, forcing them to use the carcasses of animals to cover their bones after their skin falls from their bodies."

"That's gross," Okum said with a cough.

"The secrets within the western world are vast and will need uncovering. If we're going to find our way back to Sahael, learning these secrets and using them to our advantage is key," Lyshyla said.

They traveled through the hole in the wall and entered the D.I.M Nations. Darkness soon enveloped them as stars began blinking overhead. In the distance the lights of a city glowed.

"That must be the city of Neves," Lyshyla said. "If so, we're moving exactly as I'd hoped."

"I see a farm," Oadira pointed. About a half mile away, pale candlelight could be seen through farmhouse windows. A dilapidated barn stood dark against the fading light of the sunset. "It looks like the lights are burning in the house. We can sneak inside of that barn and spend the night. I've got the first watch while all of you sleep."

"Allow me to take the first watch, Oadira," Lyshyla said as they entered the barn. It smelled of hay and rotting wood. The farm was full of pigs, sheep, goats, and chickens; inside the barn were stalls full of healthy stallions. The barn was thirty-by-forty and two-levels high.

"You will need your rest," Oadira continued. "You all need as much rest as you can get. You're outside of the eastern world, so the strength you have here is limited at best. It's finite. As a result, sleep and recovery are essential to ensure your effectiveness in western Aarde."

Ozias frowned and stroked his bearded chin. "I don't understand."

"Aarde was separated into two for reasons I've explained to you already," Lyshyla said as she sat down, looking through the doors of the barn.

Ozias kicked some hay and swore. "I'm sick of being told things only when we ask about them!"

"What do you mean?" Lyshyla asked, turning back to Ozias.

"You Educators!" he yelled. "Don't you think it would have been nice for us to know our natural abilities would be muted once we entered the western end of Aarde? Don't you think that would have been information we should have had?"

Oadira nodded her head. She had long understood Lyshyla's penchant for only offering information once the right question was asked, but sometimes they had no way of knowing whether they had asked the right thing or not, or whether there was even a question needing to be asked. It had been frustrating for 30 years, but now it was becoming dangerous.

"I need to know things so I can protect my family," Ozias fumed, staring at Lyshyla.

Oxum stepped forward, every bit as tall and formidable as Ozias. "Father," he said, placing his hand on Ozias' shoulder. "My brothers and I are strong. We've been trained to fight for the past 20 years. We don't need your protection."

"It's not about protection!" Ozias screamed. "You're not a father! I am! I am a king and a husband. I've seen my wife sacrifice and play pawn to all these prophecies and premonitions and a thousand bloodlines. Is it too much to ask to be told what we're facing once in a while? Is that too much to ask?"

His voice echoed through the barn, causing several of the penned animals to bellow in protest.

"Our entire lives seem controlled by these destinies laid out by people and gods in other realms!" he continued, spit flying from his mouth. Go to Sahael! Go to Sahael! Go to Sahael! Maybe we could if anyone gave us a straight god damn answer once in a while. We finally get a gate open and yet we're no closer to getting to our destination."

"We are---" Lyshyla tried to interject.

"We're not!" Ozias pointed an accusatory finger. "It's always more history and more waiting. I'm tired of it. How many people out there in the world died and suffered while we had to stay in Nier's Realm? I haven't spoken to my father in over 16 years. I have no idea where my friends are, or if they're alive or dead, or enslaved. I haven't been able to do anything to help anyone, and now that we're finally out and setting our sights on doing something instead of waiting around, you tell me our abilities are finite here?"

Oadira stood. She understood Ozias' anger, but it would do them no good to attack each other and give into their frustration.

"Ozias," she said, touching his hand.

Her husband pulled away. "I'm tired," he spat. "I'll find a spot of hay on the top landing and I'm going to bed. After all, I'd hate to get too tired for us to continue our journey nowhere."

Ozias stomped off, climbed a wooden ladder to the loft area, and disappeared among the rafters. His boys followed, leaving Oadira and Lyshyla alone.

Through the night, the men slept silently. Lyshyla and Oadira sat at the barn door peering out into the dark, staring at the farm animals grazing under the stars.

"I am sorry," Lyshyla said after hours of silence.

"It's alright," Oadira replied. "He has been holding onto that anger for some time. I was content in Nier's Realm if I'm being honest. I watched my sons grow up, learn to fight even better than I do, serve the people in the city of Nieth even though they weren't their people. It was peaceful. For a time, I forgot about everything going on outside the realm. Even the earthquakes that would rock the city on occasion seemed quaint in comparison to the horrors of the outside world. Ozias though…he wanted to help his people out in Aarde. He wants to see his father again and fight witan armies and free enslaved people."

"You want all those things too, my queen," Lyshyla said, eyes locked on a cow munching grass near a wooden fence.

"I do. I truly do. I guess I just have faith everything will happen as has been foreseen by prophets and deities. When I was enduring the trials for Okavango's Heart, I could only go on faith; faith in myself and faith in the mission that has been given to my family. I also think it helped me to understand that my life is going to be very long. Being in Nier's Realm for 16 years will have been a blink of an eye in my later years. I don't think Ozias has quite grasped that truth yet. To him, our sons are still children. He has a hard time seeing them as men, who if you ask me, are better fighters than he is."

Lyshyla smiled and nodded.

The cow they had been watching suddenly mooed loudly.

"Shh! There they are," Lyshyla whispered. "Just as I suspected."

To Oadira's horror, she watched as human-like creatures slunk from the darkness and grabbed the cow with rotting fingers. The bovine tried to run but was pulled to the ground by a half dozen Nethani, skin sagging from their bones. The Nethani ravaged the cow, eating it raw and using its blood-soaked hide for clothing. The sound of their feasting, grunting and lip smacking made Oadira queasy.

"Look and you will see the Nethani move about in the night," Lyshyla said. "They come from below ground using Nebuchadnezzar's obsidian portal from Necropolis to terrorize the surface dwellers of the D.I.M. Nations."

"Why are they doing this?" Oadira asked.

"For the control of Sahaedeath," Lyshyla said matter-of-factly. "Lord Commander Natas, according to Professor Nalace's journals, promised to the Nethani that after Aarde was whitewashed, the Kingdom of Sahaedeath would be given to them as long as they were fully under his control. With dominion over the dead in Aarde, the rules of magic have no effect on them since they're dead and can't be killed by conventional means."

"I hope our paths never cross," Oadira said.

Lyshyla sighed heavily as the Nethani moved toward the farmhouse.

"While they're attacking the family, it's the perfect distraction to get off this farm," Lyshyla said, standing up.

Oadira watched as the Nethani began breaking windows and pulling the door off the hinges of the dark home.

"We can't leave that family to die," Oadira hissed. She tried to form a weapon of light as she had a thousand times before, but only an anemic glow emanated from her hand.

"You see?" Lyshyla said. "You are weaker here. We cannot risk you or your family being killed simply to save a few people."

"Oadira moved to open the barn door as a scream echoed from the farmhouse. "I can't stand by and do nothing!"

Lyshyla grabbed Oadira's arm. "I know, but we can't afford to help them and expose ourselves. We have no chance against a legion of Nethani, and that is what we will have if a small group like this sees someone of the Royal Bloodline here among the D.I.M. Nations. Leaving this place before daylight is our only option. Wake up your sons."

As the family escaped into the night, the sounds of death followed them. Oadira tried to push away the screams of women and children from the farmhouse, but found they lingered long after sunrise had colored the green grasslands once more. By mid-morning, a cold rain began to fall, adding to the overall murkiness of their mental state.

They traveled cautiously, arriving at the top of the coast of Myti late the next day. As Lyshyla had warned, Oadira felt fatigue like she hadn't in years. The trek had truly drained her strength, especially with the constant wetness they experienced due to the climate weather.

Ozias, for his part, had not spoken the entire day. He stepped forward stoically, feet sloshing in his soaked boots, leading his sons though the unknown land.

His attitude had seemed to spread to his boys.

"Why are we here? Where are we going?" Oshún asked as they crested a hill on the coastline. Waves crashed against white cliffs below them.

"The Society of Secrets," Lyshyla said. "A land hidden deep inside the water straits. The only way to get in is by swimming through the water and allowing the eddy to suck us all in. It's going to take us some time to travel through the elaborate waterways until we all appear on the other side of the Only River, in the six islands of Tard."

Oshún looked at his brothers and shrugged. They returned to their grudged silence. The seven of them walked into the Aeillus Ocean, following Lyshyla as they approached the eddy down the Inler straights.

"Keep walking everyone and the eddy will suck you in naturally," Lyshyla called as she stepped into the water.

The royal family did as they were told, walking directly to the edge of the eddy. The waters were treacherous as rain fell continuously and thunder and lightning filled the Aardian skies. The wind started to grow violent, blowing in every direction, as a typhoon headed in their direction.

"Blink your eyes everyone and dive into the eddy, on the count of three. One . . . two . . . three."

They all dove simultaneously, holding each other's hands. The water was cold, but their skin soon adapted. Even in their weakened state, the water was their element and would always be a safe place for the Orishan bloodline.

As they traveled through the eddy, they experienced the speed and sudden changes of the currents. The salty water moved over Oadira's face, and for a moment she let go of Ozias and Lyshyla's hands. Images formed in her mind…visions of the past suddenly clear as if she was seeing them in front of her face at that very moment. She smelled burning bodies and heard screams.

Oadira dreamt of when she was a little girl and her mother had rushed outside of Khartoum Palace at sunset to find her playing by the waters with Aamira and Heziara. The girls didn't understand what was going on, or why they had seen people running up the steps of the palace.

"Oadira! Oadira! Oadira! Where are you?" High Queen Nergal yelled. She was so beautiful in her headdress and robes. How had Oadira forgotten how regal and powerful her mother had been?

"I'm over here," Oadira said.

Nergal hurried over to her quickly.

"I have to get you somewhere safe," her mother said. "Sahael is under attack!" Nergal grabbed Oadira's arm, hurrying and grabbing Aamira and Heziara in the process, as she ran back inside of Khartoum Palace.

Oadira then came out of her personal flashback. She could still smell the fires and see the worry on her mother's face.

Why had she suddenly seen that vision? Did it have something to do with the water? Something about the land itself? Or was it because the last stage of her mission was finally starting?

She had no idea.

The family swam for several miles under the guidance of Lyshyla until reaching their destination.

"We made it," Lyshyla said as they stepped from the water onto a beach. A dense forest encircled the sand a few dozen feet away. Waves crashed behind them.

"Let's get dry," Ozias said. "And find some food."

It was the first time he had spoken since the night before.

"Is everyone okay?" Oadira asked. The sand felt good between her toes. The rain had stopped, but the clouds overhead still stared down on them menacingly.

The group sat for a few minutes catching their breath, watching the surf roil and feeling the wind on their face. Oadira wanted to sleep. She hadn't rested since the barn, and even then, she hadn't slept at all. And she was hungry; far hungrier than she had been in quite some time.

But the snapping of a twig behind her pulled her attention from any stomach pangs.

A group of twelve guards covered in black cloaks that made them appear slightly invisible rushed from the dark forest, silent as ghosts. Several pulled throwing darts from their belts and immediately threw them toward their tired targets.

"Evasive maneuvers!" Ozias shouted.

Oadira leaped up, but before she had even attempted to conjure a sword, Oxum and Oya fell as darts hit them both in the chest.

"Oxum! Oya!" Oadira screamed as another volley of darts flew their way.

Oadira and Ozias blinked their eyes twice, making their eyes cerulean. She tried once again to form a weapon but found it too difficult. Still, with her senses heightened, time seemed to slow. The darts flew through the air, but she was able to dodge them easily, as did Ozias. Lyshyla placed herself in front of Onika to protect him.

The hooded people fired another round of darts, but Oadira, Ozias, and Oshún continued avoiding them.

Oshún, showing his natural strength, used his Orishan artes to conjure a shield to deflect the incoming darts. He then conjured several miniature spears, thrusting them in the direction of where the darts came from. The diminutive daggers pierced the chests of three of the cloaked assassins, killing them instantly.

The attackers broke ranks and split up, making it more difficult for Oshún to hit them. They moved with great skill and speed, obviously trained well in their craft.

Seeing that their son had been successful in conjuring small weapons, Oadira and Ozias did the same. They continued dodging darts while using their Orishan artes to manifest small daggers of light and sending them flying in all directions, hitting multiple assassins.

"Father!" Oshún cried out as he was hit by several poisoned barbs and fell unconscious.

"Oshún!" Ozias shouted.

Dodging a volley of darts, Oadira charged at the line of cloaked men. Rage engulfed her entire mind and body. She grabbed the closest attacker by his hood before snapping his neck like a dry twig. Despite her fatigue and the difficulty of manifesting mental weapons, she invoked a short sword and plunged it into the neck of the next assassin. She moved as if through water, feeling slow and sluggish, but even so, she killed two others before freezing rain began pelting her shoulders and neck. She turned in surprise.

Ozias, seeing that Oadira was weakening, used his Orishan powers to manipulate the water, turning it into an icy rain that made the assailants step back and look to the skies that a moment ago had been clear and blue.

The darts stopped being thrown.

Oadira stumbled back, overcome by exhaustion. She saw three of her four sons limp in the sand but had no strength to crawl over to check on them.

"Who are you, and why have you come?" a hooded man asked. Lyshyla quickly came forward, but Oadira silently raised her hand, forcing Lyshyla to step back.

"Maybe you should've asked us that first before attacking us without warning!" Oadira said in a fit of rage.

"Apologies!" the man said, stepping forward from the remaining assassins. "The last time we had visitors, they attacked and destroying our city, killing many."

"I understand. But we're here to find a way back to Sahael," Oadira answered, still too tired to stand.

The guard removed his cloak and hood. Dreadlocks hung past his shoulders, framing a square jaw and angular features. He stepped toward Oadira with his hands out in a peaceful gesture. He stopped suddenly, staring at her bright blue eyes. With a gasp, he dropped to one knee and bowed his head.

"The Times are upon us," the man said. He rose to his feet with a look of urgency upon his face. "Who are you?"

"Queen Oadira of Iceoth," Oadira nodded, catching her breath. "Daughter of High Queen Nergal of Sahael. Keeper of Okavango's Heart. Empress of Neir's Realm."

The assassins collectively gasped and murmured together.

Ozias stood rigidly beside his sons, eyes burning into the assassins. "I am King Ozias, and these are my sons you have attacked!"

Their leader nodded quickly, dreadlocks spilling over his shoulder. "You all must come with us, quickly."

"It's best we follow them," Lyshyla said, still standing in front of Onika.

"We won't go anywhere with you!" Ozias shouted, forming another pair of daggers in his hands. Sweat dripped from his nose, evidence of the effort required to use his abilities. "You've hurt my sons!"

"Again, apologies," the man said. He motioned for one of his fellow assassins to step forward. "They have only been hit with a mild sedative. We had no intention of killing anyone." He turned and pointed at his five dead colleagues lying in the bloody sand. "And we have paid for our assault with blood. But let me make it right. We have an herb that when smelled, will revive them. Please, let my fellow soldier help your children."

Ozias looked at Oadira and she nodded.

"Do it," Ozias ordered.

The assassin stepped forward and pulled what looked like a cinnamon stick from his belt. He held it under each of the boy's noses one after the other. Slowly their eyes began to flutter.

"Where would you be taking us?" Oadira breathed as she stood shakily.

"The city of Synagogue," the man said. "Home to all assassins, and the SOS."

"SOS? What do those letters stand for?" Oadira asked, helping Oshún and her other sons to their feet.

"If you don't know, then you'll never know. We are forbidden to share such knowledge," one of the hooded men said.

"The Society of Secrets, assassins who share the blood of the ancients," Lyshyla answered.

"You are an Educator," the man said, nodding to Lyshyla.

"I am Educator Lyshyla, formerly of Timbuktu, the court of King Nilhist of Iceoth, and the royal palace of Neith in Nier's Realm."

"What is your name, soldier?" Oadira asked the lead assassin.

"His name is Scion," Lyshyla said. "If he is truly of the Society of Secrets, all the males and females are named Scion. It's the name they all go by, remaining one in body, mind, and spirit with one objective and single purpose. The purpose of their order was keeping a watchful eye over the Ancient Bloodlines, remaining in the shadows to always ensure their safety. The sooner we can get to Synagogue City, the better."

“I am Scion,” the man nodded. “We are all Scion. Now, we must go.”

Wearily, Oadira, Ozias, and their sons followed the assassins into the forest. Several of them dragged their dead comrades from the beach, leaving them in a crook of a large tree and covering them with leaves.

“We shall return later to bury our comrades,” Scion said. “For now, speed is our ally.”

After traveling for an hour through the dense jungle, the royal family finally arrived in Synagogue City, a place of ruined beauty. The city had pillars that held up what was left of a destroyed Woodstone buildings. Everything appeared to be made from quartz and petrified wood with brown and cream circles naturally adorning the walls. Lakes, rivers, and Marula Trees surrounded what remained of Synagogue, while mountains and clouds framed the scene. Fish swam in the waters, birds filled the skies, and animals roamed the marshes. People in colorful robes moved about trading and rebuilding. Women passed them carrying bundles of clothing or large pitchers of water on their heads. Some looked at the newcomers with curiosity; others seemed oblivious to the royal family walking in their midst.

“This place has been through hell,” Lyshyla whispered.

“As I said,” Scion replied, “we have been through much.”

Scion led them to a large rectangular building lined with pillars and tall marble statues painted with vibrant pigments. The building showed signs of having been rebuilt, with patched cracks still running up many of the walls. Scion ran inside and returned after a moment with a tall man dressed in flowing robes of scarlet, gold, and emerald. Closely cropped white hair covered his head, and his lined face seemed quick to smile. Three women walked behind him wearing similar robes and golden bracelets. Each woman stood six-feet-five-inches tall. The three of them were slender with athletic frames, long, braided hair, ivory teeth and beautiful, walnut skin. They were distinguished by the color of their eyebrows: one possessed black tourmaline eyebrows and eyes, the second emerald tsavorite eyebrows and eyes, and the third possessed gray labradorite-colored eyebrows and eyes.

"Educator Nortan," Scion began, addressing the old man. "This is Queen Oadira, keeper of Okavango's Heart and heir to Sahael. This is King Ozias and their four sons, along with Educator Lyshyla."

"Welcome to Synagogue City," Educator Nortan said with a bow. "The signs of the Times are upon us. You are welcome here, Oadira of Sahael. Allow me to introduce the Bastards of Royalty, Sy with her sisters Ky and Ny."

"Bastards of Royalty?" Oadira questioned. She had never heard of any such title before, let alone someone using the term 'bastard' as something positive.

"Yes," Educator Nortan replied. "This must sound strange to outsiders, though I am sure Educator Lyshyla is aware of the importance of these lovely women. They are the Bastards of Royalty, children of the ancient seed born out of wedlock and sent to the Society per the Nairobi laws, to be trained as assassins to look after the bloodlines of Sahael, Egyptus, and the Horn." Nortan stepped to the side and waved his arm slowly toward the woman with the black eyebrows and eyes, then the emerald, and finally the gray. "Sy, First Leader of the Society; Ky, Second Leader of the Society; Ny, Third Leader of the Society, and Fourth Leader Fy who isn't present. They're the bastards from the lands of Sahael, Egyptus, and the Horn. They were identical quintuplets by chance, blessed by Ibeji with four distinct bloodlines. The Sahaelian bloodline, the Egyptus bloodline, and the Horn bloodline, to serve the Ancient Families in Alkebulan."

"What brings you through the Inler Straights to Synagogue

City?" First leader Sy asked Oadira, voice sweet but powerful.

"We're in need of your assistance," Oadira answered.

"Why should we help you?" Second Leader Ky asked with a slight smirk on her face. Her voice sounded identical to that of her sister.

"Because you're of the Ancient, Egyptian, and Moorish bloodlines, it's your obligation to help us," Lyshyla said sharply.

"We ask you again: what brings you here?" First Leader Sy repeated.

"There has to be a specific reason," Second Leader Ky said, rubbing her hands together.

"Yes," Third Leader Ny agreed, voice exactly the same as her two sisters. "We would like a reason, and we are deserving of such."

"What is this?" Ozias spat. "You're supposed to help us!"

"Ozias," Odira said, eyes locked on the three women. "Calm yourself."

"Yes, King Ozias," First leader Sy said with a hint of disdain. "Calm yourself."

"I would have you explain yourselves instead," Educator Nortan smiled, though his eyes remained hard.

Lyshyla gave a soft bow before Educator Nortan and the three women, commanding respect.

"We apologize for our intrusion in your land," Lyshyla said, stepping in front of Ozias. "The Signs of the Times are the reason we're here. The currents are changing Aarde for reasons we can't fully understand. The sooner we can get to Sahael, the sooner we can find out what's really going on."

"It's true," First Commander Sy said as her Tourmaline

eyebrows and eyes got wide.

"The Signs of the Times are truly upon us," Second Leader Ky said.

"We've noticed and could feel the changes in the waters," First leader Sy nodded. "The waters of the eddy reversed course, allowing you entry. It's the only possible way an Orisha can make it to our home safely traveling through the western waters of Aarde, one of the many secrets in the western world."

"It was prophesied years ago that an Orishan heir would allow us the ability to regain our honor and standing, paving the way for us to return back to Sahael, and upholding our rightful duties," Ny said.

"Regain your honor and standing, paving a way back to Sahael?" Oadira asked.

"The Society of Secrets was formed by the Educators of Timbuktu before the fall of Sahael," Lyshyla replied, staring straight ahead at First leader Sy. "The purpose of the Society was to find information and clues about Sahael, Alkebulan, and its peoples. They were working in secret to help the Educators gather mysteries about the royal families in Sahael. After working on behalf of the Educators, friction was created after the Society discovered uncomfortable information about themselves regarding the Sahaelians, Egyptians, and the Hornans."

"Yes," Second Leader Ky interrupted. "We discovered that we're the rejected offspring of the royal families who birthed children out of wedlock in Sahael, Egyptus, and the Horn. According to the Nairobi laws, only the four chosen heirs of Sahael can have children to create succession among their bloodlines. When sexual pleasures within the bloodline are performed without the proper rights, there are significant ramifications."

"Rather than killing us off," Third Leader Ny continued as

if speaking in place of her sister. “Solomon and the Educators persuaded the four families to create a law that allowed Sahael, Egyptus, and the Horn the ability to send the children through the Inler straits to be trained as assassins, ensuring they were to have no recollection of who or what they are.”

“Then how did you find out about all of this?” Oadira asked.

“Lord Commander Natas and the Narsans visited and promised to help us understand who we really were if we agreed to help him,” First Leader Sy said.

Oadira’s fists clenched. If they knew who they were, that meant they had helped Natas attack Sahael and all the other free lands. She felt the distinct impression they weren’t safe here.

“What did Natas do to convince you?” Lyshyla asked.

Educator Nortan stepped forward. “Lord Commander Natas convinced the four leaders of their bloodlines, explaining to them they were of royal blood. I confirmed to them that everything the Lord Commander said was truthful. Lord Commander Natas brought me records and then took Sy, Ny, Fy, and Ky to the historical narratives of their people,”

“I remember seeing you there,” First Leader Sy said, pointing to Lyshyla. “You were an instructor of the Lord Commander, if I remember correctly.”

“You remember correctly,” Lyshyla said as she pressed her lips together. “Do you all remember what I taught you?”

“You taught us that we were the rejected bastards of royal families kept in secret to hide their shame,” First Leader Sy said. “You said that we were a summation of all of their previously hidden mistakes and forgotten.”

Second Leader Ky continued. “Lord Commander Natas made it clear that the bloodlines of Sahael possessed talents and gifts that could be unlocked within each of our bloodlines. He chose to help us unlock our cloaking abilities. Lord Commander Natas tasked my sisters and I with operating in the shadows, working in the confines of the great powers in Alkebulan."

"For what reasons?" Lyshyla asked.

Third Leader Ny looked directly at Oadira. "Revenge."

Oadira sprang forward, feeling a renewed sense of energy as rage engulfed her. "You took advantage of the Educators and used what you were taught and then started working for Lord Commander Natas?"

"We did," First Leader Sy replied.

"That knowledge you acquired was given freely!" Lyshyla shouted, seemingly as angry as Oadira. "Being of ancient blood, you're bound by the Nairobi laws."

"That is correct," First leader Sy said as she nodded her head in agreement.

"We did by easily manipulating our way through Sahael, infiltrating from the inside." Second Leader Ky said.

Lyshyla's eyes grew wide. "All three of you saw it happening and share responsibility for Sahael's downfall! You helped Lord Commander Natas infiltrate, kill, and enslave millions. The Society is responsible for the great dispersion and scattering of the Diaspora!"

First Leader Sy stood tall, back stretched as she seemed to tower over Lyshyla. "We were rejected and despised by our own flesh and blood! If not for Lord Commander Natas, we wouldn't be here today. Our bodies would have been thrown in mass graves like the other rejected babies that never reached full growth. We had every right and are justified in the role we played in Sahael's destruction. What was done to us should never have taken place, and the people of Sahael deserved every penalty that came upon them at the hands of Lord Commander Natas!"

Oadira wanted to conjure a blade and decapitate the women standing before her, but she also understood their resentment. Something else stayed her hand as well; a single tear fell down First Leader Sy's dark cheek.

"But we were not supported by Lord Commander Natas after our efforts," Sy spoke calmly. "It wasn't until after Sahael's destruction that he turned on us as well, trying to kill all of us to tie up loose ends. It forced my sisters and I to close our borders, allowing us to remain isolated from western Aarde."

Second Leader Ky continued. "Educator Nortan helped us come to the error of our ways and taught us how Lord Commander Natas manipulated us to further his own agenda. We didn't really understand the damage created by our actions, which forced us into hiding for decades."

"You are the first outsiders to make it here since our arrival," Third Leader Ny said. "As soon as the currents started to change and reverse in the opposite direction, that's when we knew we had a chance at redemption."

"And what are you all willing to do to regain redemption?" Lyshyla asked.

"The Times are upon us," Educator Nortan replied. "And there is much that needs to be done. We have the means to get you back to Sahael, but we would need something in return if these daughters were to help you do it."

"And what is that?" Oadira asked. "It seems there's always a price in these things. Perhaps one day we'll meet someone who has no hidden agenda that must be met before they will allow us to help other people." She looked at First Leader Sy. "But today is not that day, and I would expect nothing less from someone like you who betrayed innocents just to make themselves feel better."

"Our actions brought us no joy in the end," First Leader Sy said.

"And I'm overjoyed to hear it," Oadira spat. She turned to Educator Nortan. "What is your price?"

"You will not like it," the old man nodded.

"Why not?"

"Because the price…is high."

[To be continued on Volume 1 Book 5]

OUT NOW:

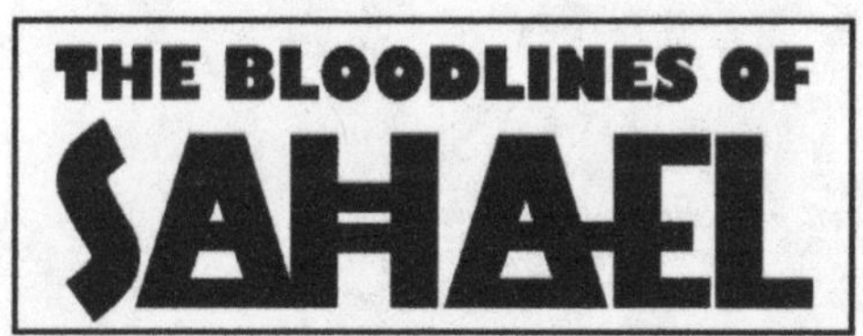

VOLUME ONE

BOOK FIVE

THE ORISHA OF SAHAEL

www.ingramcontent.com/pod-product-compliance
Lightning Source LLC
Chambersburg PA
CBHW010448310726
48979CB00018B/2854/J

* 9 7 8 1 9 6 3 0 8 9 0 3 5 *